Jainism
AT A
GLANCE

A Religion of Non-violence

SUBHASH C. JAIN

Front Jacket Caption: Shri Ashtapadji, supposedly situated in the snow-covered mountains of the Himalayas, houses 24 idols of Tirthankaras made of gemstones. Reproduced with permission from the Jain Center of America, Inc., New York.

Printed by CreateSpace
Charleston, SC

Visit www.createspace.com/3450849 to order additional copies.

ISBN: 1452841853
ISBN-13: 9781452841854

Contents

Appendices

Preface

This book is targeted at young Jains, especially those who were born and/or raised outside India. My objective in writing this book is to familiarize the emerging generation of Jains with the fundamental concepts of Jainism.

Jainism proves that there exists a successful and eco-logically responsible way of life which is abundantly non-violent in thought, action, and deed. Accordingly, one who neglects or disregards the existence of earth, air, fire, water, and vegetation disregards his own existence, which is en-twined with them.

Author Michael Tobias notes:

> *Jainism provides penetrating insights into ethical realism, phenomenal integrity, and child-like ideal-ism—unblushing, naked, powerful, and enduring. Jainism absolutely changed the course of the sub-continent. Its aesthetic principles altered the mindset, religious devotion, and daily life of tens of millions. It is an arguable point among scholars, yet there is good reason to reflect that eight hundred million Hindus today trace their orthodoxy—with its own reverence for life and stated vegetarianism—not to Brahmanic, but rather sramanic tradition, namely, to the ancient Jain ascetics whose sculptured remnants have turned up in the archeological finds in the Indus Valley civilization.*

Material included in this book has been presented in the past by different scholars of Jainism. With that in mind, what I have said in the book is nothing new. My contribution has been limited to explaining various Jain concepts and philosophies in a manner that will enable and encourage readers detached from the mainstream of life of Jains in India—to grasp the concepts without undue effort.

I am indebted to the authors of books and articles on Jainism whose ideas have been the foundation of this book. If I have misinterpreted their points of view, it reflects my limitation as a student of Jainism, and I take full responsibility for that. I sincerely thank my friends and relatives who were kind enough to read the initial drafts of the manuscript and make numerous suggestions for improvement and accurate presentation of Jain concepts and philosophies. My wife Sadhna and our children, Aarti and Amit, have been a great source of inspiration to me in undertaking this task, and finishing it on time. Without their support and encouragement, it would have been impossible to complete it.

I am indebted to the talented members of my editorial team at CreateSpace for their role in the shaping of the book. Whitney Parks, Lead Publishing consultant at the company, furnished excellent advice on the structure of the book.

A special mention of appreciation must go to Michele Metcalf and Shayna Mesko in my office, for preparing the final manuscript. I owe a special word of gratitude to Chris Earley (Dean of the Business School, University of Connecticut) who encouraged me to undertake this project.

I humbly take full responsibility for any errors of omission and commission.

Mahavira Jayanti (Birth), 2010   Subhash C. Jain

Chapter One

The Concept of Jainism

*I adore so greatly the principles of the Jain religion that
I would like to be reborn in a Jain Community.*
—George Bernard Shaw

Jainism is an ancient religion. Its thorough emphasis on personal and societal nonviolence in thought, speech, and action has significantly influenced world peace. Jains share the primary goal of unconditional love with a commitment to respect all forms of life. The wisdom of Jainism has inspired many peaceful revolutionaries, including Mahatma Gandhi and Martin Luther King, Jr. According to historians and to archaeological evidence, the Jain tradition has flourished within the Indian subcontinent for over 8,000 years. Followers of Jainism point to evidence of its being much older.

The word *Jain* is derived from *Jina*, which means spiritual conqueror. Followers of Jina are called Jains. Jinas are individuals who have overcome or conquered their inner enemies, the flaws and weaknesses, and the attachments and aversions that prevent one from achieving one's infinite spiritual potential and have realized inherent supreme knowledge. Jains revere twenty-four Jinas called *Tirthankaras* who taught the Jain message to the human race during various periods of antiquity.

Although Jainism is the oldest religion in the world, historical knowledge of the faith is traced to the last of the twenty-four Tirthankaras, Lord Mahavira, who lived in the sixth century BC. Hindu religious texts make reference to twenty-three other Jain Tirthankaras who existed before Lord Mahavira. There are specific references made to the first Jain Tirthankara, Lord Adinatha, in many Hindu treatises.

The basic thesis of Jainism is that all living beings seek happiness which can be achieved only through total liberation from this world. Liberation is achieved by freeing the soul from *all Karmas*, both good and bad. Although all followers of Jainism have total liberation as their goal, it is difficult to attain. Nonetheless, even laypeople should not disregard the ultimate goal of total liberation.

In practice, a layperson should be more concerned with eliminating bad Karmas and maximizing good Karmas in order to enhance both well-being in this life and the chances of a better rebirth. Jains, therefore, embrace a wide range of ascetic and devotional activities and practice rigorous asceticism to a feasible extent. This is why a typical Jain leads a more austere life than other Indians.

Jain monks, however, engage in single-minded pursuit of liberation. They depend on laypeople to provide shelter, food, clothing, books, and ritual paraphernalia (for example, a thread to embroider the cloth that covers the handles of the brooms each monk carries to sweep away insects). The monks are peripatetic because staying in one place may lead to attachment.

Jainism emphasizes the central role of the individual. You cannot save the world, but you can cultivate your own garden—which the Jains know to be the soul.

Chapter Two

Antiquity of Jainism

Sympathy for the lowest animals is one of the noblest virtues with which man is endowed.

—Charles Darwin

Based on historical references and archaeological evidence, Jainism may accurately be called an ancient religion. Some scholars consider it to be the oldest religion. It was founded by the first Tirthankara Rishabhanatha or Adinatha. It preceded the Vedic religion that forms the basis of Hinduism. Before further dealing with the origins of Jainism, it is desirable to trace the history of Indian civilization.

Indian Civilization

Much has been said and written about ancient India. At the cost of oversimplification, the Indian civilization can be classified into five time periods:

1) Mehrgarh Era (around 8000 BC): The Mehrgarh is located in the Bolan Pass region of Baluchistan, now in Pakistan.
2) Sarasvati Era (around 7000-1900 BC): The Sarasvati era refers to civilization that developed in the region of the River Sarasvati that flowed through Rajasthan and poured into the Gulf of Kutch near the Kathiawar peninsula.

3) Harappa and Mohenjo-Daro Era (3000-1900 BC): Civilization that existed along the Indus River.
4) Vedic Civilization (1900-500 BC).
5) Historical Times (500 BC onward): As an example, Tirthankara Mahavira's time (599-527 BC).

Up to 1922, the Indian civilization had been traced to the Vedic period. But in 1922, archaeological excavations unearthed the ruins of an advanced civilization in the Indus valley region with two urban centers, at Harappa and Mohenjo-Daro. This civilization had developed rich agricultural tracts throughout the region and had built a sophisticated urban and literate culture.

Certain ancient scales and seals from Harappa and Mohenjo-daro finds show the nude posture of the body and the pose of the eyes being riveted on the tips of the noses in the figures resembling Tirthankara Rishabhanatha. The actual readings of these seals bearing such words such as "Risabha Nama" show that Tirthankara Rishabhanatha was worshipped in the area some 5,000 years ago.

It is interesting to note that though many objects of interest were found in the excavations, no weapons of protective ramparts or fortifications were discovered. Thus, it may be presumed Jain culture prevailed in that region over 8,000 years ago. If the first Tirthankara was worshipped in the Harappa and Mohenjo-Daro time, he must have been born prior to that time.

The discovery of Mohenjo-Daro on the west bank of the Indus River, some 200 miles from the shores of the Arabian Sea and of the Harappa about 350 miles further north, encouraged archaeologists to look for other sites along the fertile banks of the Indus. Their efforts led to the discovery of other sites such as Chanhu Paro, Amri, and Kot Diji. These sites were considered to be a part of the Indus civilization.

Further excavations revealed that many more sites are located not along the Indus but in the middle of the desert. But how did these towns buried under mountains of sand flourish? Satellite photos revealed that today's Great Indian Desert was once traversed by a river with its own fertile banks. Geologists identified this river as the Sarasvati River, reinforced by mention in the Vedic Scriptures. The Sarasvati River flowed from the Tibetan Himalayas into the Arabian Sea, covering a distance similar to the Indus.

The Sarasvati was the mightiest of all the rivers of northern India, and had been praised in the Rig-Veda in the following words:

> *She, Sarasvati flows with a nourishing stream, Sarasvati, for our support, like a cooper fort. In her greatness the river drives away, like a charioteer, all other (rivers). Unique among rivers, Sarasvati flows from the mountains to the ocean. Revealing wealth and the world's abundances, she has yielded milk and ghee [i.e., purified butter], for (King) Nahusha (and his descendants).*

Origin of Jainism

It will be reasonable to assume that Tirthankara Rishabhanatha was born in the Sarasvati region around 6,000 BC. It is in that time period that Jainism originated. Tirthankara Adinathan's time period can be corroborated in another way. Students of Indic civilization claim that Lord Krishna lived sometime between 1200 to 1000 BC and that Tirthankara Neminatha, the twenty-second Tirthankara, was his cousin who lived during the same time period. Assuming one Tirthankara was born every 200 years prior to 1200 BC, Tirthankara Rishabhanatha must have lived sometime around 6,000 BC. Thus, it can be safely assumed that Tirthankara Adinathatha belonged to the Sarasvati era.

Since Jainism has flourished from times immemorial in the context of Indic civilization, it is important that readers have some insights into the history, philosophy, politics, and economics of this great civilization. Although the five time periods of the Indic civilization were identified at the beginning of this chapter, Appendix A at the end provides an overview of the civilization from antiquity to the modern day.

The Hindu literature accepts the fact that Jainism was founded by Rishabhanatha, and placed his time almost at what they conceived to be the commencement of world civilization, which could be considered the Sarasvati era. The Hindu literature gave Rishabhanatha the same parentage (father Nabhiraja and mother Marudevi) the Jains do. Also, it is commonly agreed that after the name of Rishabhanatha's oldest son Bharata, India had been known as Bharata-Varsa.

Chapter Three

Jain Philosophy

All the evils of the world owe their origin to
"Rag and Dwesh," predation and greed.[1]

According to Jainism there are six entities in the universe: one living entity—the soul—and five nonliving entities—matter and energy, motion, rest, space, and time. An immortal and indestructible soul resides in every living being. The living entity can be classified into worldly souls and liberated souls.

Worldly souls interact with matter and energy of various kinds. This interaction leads to actions of body, mind, and speech in the context of motion, rest, space, and time. The actions give birth to *Karmas*. Karmas, in Jainism, are particles of matter that become attached to the soul and cannot be removed by senses or instruments. All living entities carry Karma particles from one life to the next. The cycle of birth and death continues forever, and the suffering never ends. Karmas can be good or bad, depending on the state of mind of an individual. If one develops equanimity—calmness, serenity, composure—the Karmas are good. If, however, the person suffers from anger, ego, greed, deceit, or pride, the Karmas are bad. In the daily life of a layperson, good and bad Karmas are generated simultaneously.

It is the bondage of Karmas with the soul that is the root cause of a person's suffering. Under the influence of

---

1 *This quotation as well as those that follow at the beginning of each chapter are taken from various Jain scriptures.*

Karmas, the soul tends to seek pleasures in materialistic belongings and possessions. Such a self-centered perspective leads to violent thoughts and deeds, anger, hatred, greed, and other vices, which result in further accumulation of Karmas.

The doctrine of Karma occupies a significant position in the Jain philosophy. It provides a rational and satisfactory explanation for the apparently inexplicable phenomena of birth and death, happiness and misery, disparate mental and physical abilities, and the existence of different species of living beings. Karma is the principle governing the succession of life. Our actions of body, mind, and speech bind us to the Karmas.

Karmas are part of a living soul's life. Good Karmas are preferable to bad Karmas because good Karmas shed bad Karmas and because good Karmas lead to a more satisfying life. Ultimately, of course, both good and bad Karmas must be completely shed for lasting happiness. When the soul is completely free of all Karmas, it is purified and liberated. Only humans have the capacity to shed all Karmas and become liberated. In this respect, human life is the highest form of life. The essence of Jain philosophy is depicted in illustration 1.

Today, no idea is acceptable unless it meets the test of scientific reason. In this respect, Jainism is on safe ground. From the beginning, Jain thinkers have emphasized the importance of reason in all matters connected with religion. Jainism prescribes complete freedom from popular superstition as the first condition for religious development. According to Jain scholars, rational belief requires freedom from these types of superstitious faith: faith in deities, angels and demons, and faith in deluding preachers. Believing that bathing in a particular river will wash off one's sins, that circling a particular tree will promote one's virtues, or that climbing a particular hill will produce spiritual development are the kinds of mistaken ideas that must be avoided on the way of true belief in the nature of reality.

When there is an epidemic, some people try to appease the deities by offering animal sacrifices. Such an attempt to propitiate certain deities is based on the false belief that these deities are the real cause of the epidemic. Such a belief is ruinous to a society and should be eradicated. Some crooks wear the robes of monks and trade on the simplicity of the ignorant. They mislead people to secure benefits for themselves only. We must be cautious of them.

Jainism clearly prescribes that right or rational belief is the first step toward spiritual development. Thus, Jainism is in complete agreement with modern science, which insists that theories must be provable.

The Soul

A soul is a living entity. The distinguishing characteristic of a soul is consciousness. The soul fills the entire body of a living being, and the life processes of a living body take place because of the presence of the soul. When the soul leaves the body, the living being dies. The soul, then, assumes another body.

Illustration 1
Essence of Jain Philosophy

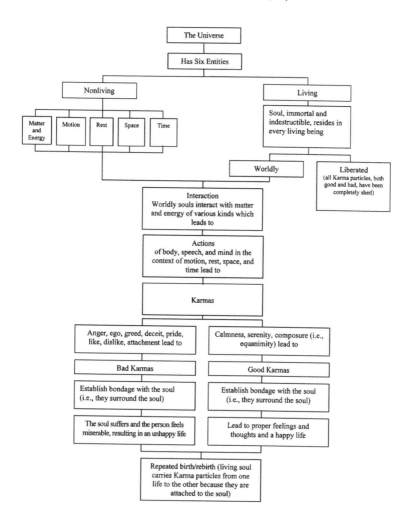

Living beings can be classified into two categories: immobile and mobile. Immobile living beings have only one sense, the sense of touch. The five kinds of immobile living beings are identified as earth-bodied, water-bodied, fire-bodied, air-bodied, and vegetable-bodied. Mobile living beings have two or more senses: those with two senses have touch and taste; those with three senses have touch, taste, and smell; those with four senses have touch, taste, smell, and sight; and those with five senses have touch, taste, smell, sight, and hearing.

The higher forms of life—humans and animals—have all five senses. Only human beings have an additional characteristic, the faculty of thinking.

Karma

The Karma particles acquired by a living being become attached to the soul. The particles that a worldly soul possesses lead to happiness or misery. This is known as Karmas bearing fruits.

The Karma particles have four features: species or nature (the kind of Karma); quantity (the amount of Karma); duration (the amount of time that Karma particles remain attached to the soul); and intensity (severity of fruition).

Thoughts involving violence, revenge, dishonesty, and other undesirable feelings lead to the influx of bad Karmas. Thoughts involving compassion, friendship, a desire to help others, and other similar feelings generate good Karmas. The quantity of Karma (good or bad) depends on the frequency with which an individual engages in thoughts giving rise to good or bad Karma. The duration of bondage of Karma particles and the intensity of fruition are determined by the passion of the individual. There-fore, the greater the intensity of passion, anger, ego, deceit, or greed in the individual, the longer the duration of the Karma, and the more severe the consequences of the Karma. The fruition of Karma leads to good and bad feelings and thoughts in an individual. These thoughts and feelings result in further influx and bondage of Karmas. This process of interaction between a soul and Karma particles is one of action and reaction. If by controlling undesirable thoughts and feelings one does not react to the fruition of Karma, the Karmic effect can be avoided.

The Jain theory of Karma is very logical for a variety of reasons. First, it is based on the idea of cause and effect. Once we accept the belief that universal phenomena are governed by the law of causation, we rule out the existence of any outside agency to govern the course of our lives. Second, it is based on the premise that association of the worldly souls and Karmic particles is eternal. The worldly souls themselves are instrumental in acquiring new Karmas, in suffering the consequences of Karmas in their possession, and in shedding Karmic particles. This cause-and-effect relationship between souls and Karmas is the main focus of the theory of causation. An important implication of the Jain theory of Karma is that there is no need for the idea of a creator, sustainer, and destroyer of the universe. Third, it rules out the intervention of gods or goddesses to protect us from calamities. Therefore, rituals of propitiation are of little value. Jainism insists on self-reliance and asks persons to develop their own moral character and pursue the path of spiritualism to free themselves from the effects of past Karmas.

The law of Karma in spiritual science is not very different from the law of action and reaction in physics. People have to correct the wrongs they have done in the past or suffer the consequences. If everyone realized that one day he or she was going to bear the consequences of his or her actions, no one would dare to indulge in anything that would hurt others.

Jain scholars have identified eight kinds of Karma particles. They are:

- Perception-obscuring Karma
- Knowledge-obscuring Karma
- Deluding Karma
- Obstructing Karma
- Feeling-producing Karma
- Life span-determining Karma
- Physique-determining Karma
- Status-determining Karma

The first four types of Karma—perception-obscuring, knowledge-obscuring, deluding, and obstructing—cover the intrinsic attributes of a soul. An individual becomes omniscient on shedding these Karmas. The remaining four Karmas—feeling-producing, life span-determining, physique-determining, and status-determining—influence the physical existence of a living being.

Ordinarily the word Karma means action. In Jainism, however, Karma has a different meaning. According to Jain principles, the combined activity of body, speech, and mind constitutes *abstract* Karma, while the extremely fine particles of matter that are associated with the worldly souls are called *material* Karma. The abstract Karma generates material Karma, which bonds with the soul. Further, three kinds of cognitive faculty precede the abstract Karma: the demeritorious cognitive faculty causing the influx of de-merit Karma, the meritorious cognitive faculty responsible for the influx of merit Karma, and the pure cognitive fac-ulty that helps the individual stop the influx of Karma and shed the Karma associated with his or her soul.

All the daily routines of life involve actions of body, speech, and mind. These routines are steered by desires, which in turn give rise to attachment and aversion, and ul-timately result in passions of anger, pride, deceit, and greed. In other words, passions play a pivotal role in our routines. The consequences include the generation of Karmas, re-sulting in pleasure and pain, success and failure, happiness and misery.

The Jain theory of Karma represents a rational system that complies with all the above requisites of the system of our routines and consequences. According to Jainism, the universe is filled with extremely fine particles of mat-ter known as Karmic particles. These Karmic particles are similar to subatomic particles like electrons, protons, and neutron, except that they are much finer than the known subatomic particles. These particles have the ability to at-tach to, and detach from, worldly souls. Thus the system of routines and consequences utilizes the notion of attach-ment and detachment of Karmic particles. The Karmic par-ticles associated with a worldly soul carry the imprints of the consequences of past actions. Modern scientific con-cepts indicate that material particles have tremendous en-ergy and can travel very fast. Karmic particles associated with a worldly soul travel with the soul. Further, they are responsible for carrying the information about the consequences of past routines of the worldly soul from one life to the next.

The entire process can be summarized as follows:

It is because of the actions of mind, body, and speech that Karmic particles become attached to the soul and are transformed into different species of Karmas. Good actions cause the attachment of beneficial species and bad actions cause the attachment of harmful species. The different species of Karmic particles remain associated with the soul for varying durations and are detached from the soul after executing the consequences.

This statement raises a question: How do Karmic particles transform into different species with different durations? How is the information about the species and duration of Karma "stored" in material Karmic particles?

The transformation of Karmic particles into appropriate species and duration is similar to a process familiar to every individual. It is a well-known fact that particles of food ingested by a living being get transformed into different constituents of the body. Food particles are inanimate and so have no knowledge about the transformations, but these transformations occur because of the intrinsic attributes of matter—atoms and molecules—and because of their environment. All transformations follow the universal laws of nature. Possibly, the species and duration of Karma particles are coded in ways similar to the code of the memory chip of a computer or the genetic code contained in DNA. The species or nature of Karmas and their respective duration depends on the nature and intensity of actions and passions.

Liberation of the Soul

The painful process of birth-death of living beings continues and leads to misery and unhappiness. To acquire true and lasting happiness, the cycle of birth and rebirth must be broken. This can be achieved by purifying the soul and thereby gaining liberation. Liberation is realized by shedding all good and bad Karmas. Ultimately, through liberation a soul achieves *Nirvana,* i.e., freedom from all suffering.

While Nirvana is a pious goal to which all human beings should aspire, achieving it may not be realistic in the modern world. Yet, even if total purification of the soul is not feasible, one should aim at generating as many good, or pure, Karmas as possible because such Karmas act to minimize the influx of bad Karmas, and thus lead to a satisfying life.

Three forces determine the kind of Karmas generated. Right perception (right faith), right knowledge, and right conduct generate good Karmas—and the opposite is also true. In this respect, Jainism differs from other religions, some of which emphasize knowledge while others emphasize conduct. Some consider faith or devotion alone enough to lead to salvation; others preach that knowledge alone is sufficient to achieve salvation. And yet others emphasize that conduct or activity alone is enough to secure salvation. Such one-sided beliefs are dismissed by the Jain thinkers who maintain that all three—perception (faith), knowledge, and conduct—must be present to achieve Nirvana.

The point may be illustrated with reference to a sick person who wants to return to good health. For this to happen, the sick man must have implicit faith in the doctor he consults. He must have a clear knowledge of the medicine or regimen prescribed by the doctor, and he must take the medicine or follow the regimen according to the instructions given by the doctor. All these three—faith in the doctor, knowledge of the medicine, and following the prescription—are necessary to eradicate the sickness and return to good health. The steps for acquiring spiritual health are the same and can only be secured by the cooperation of the three jewels of Jainism: the right faith (or perception), the right knowledge, and the right conduct.

To summarize, Jainism believes that there are nine aspects of reality. They are living being, nonliving being, influx of Karma particles, bondage of Karma particles, meritorious Karma, demeritorious Karma, stoppage of influx of Karma particles, shedding of Karma particles, and salvation.

Chapter Four

Tırthankaras (Pathfınders)

There is no greater lasting source of joy than in the saving of an animal's life; the extending of one's aid to the needy.

According to the Jain faith, since the beginning, twenty-four Tirthankaras (pathfinders or spiritual victors or conquerors of the self) have been born. Illustration 2 lists the names of the twenty-four Tirthankaras, and their cognizances (symbols used for identifying the Tirthankaras). Also shown are the trees associated with the twenty-four Tirthankaras. All the Tirthankaras gained *Kevalajnana* (right knowledge) while meditating under a tree. Therefore, these tress are sacred to Jains.

These individuals, through right perception, right knowledge, and right conduct achieved perfection in their lifetimes. They then wandered from place to place to serve as religious teachers for laymen and laywomen. On death, they achieved Nirvana, that is, freedom from birth and death.[2] Jains follow the teachings of the twenty-four Tirthankaras. The word *Tirthankar* is derived from the Sanskrit word *Teerth*, meaning a ford, the place where a person may cross the river of worldly existence and suffering.

The first twenty-two Tirthankaras in illustration 2, from Adinatha to Neminatha, belong to prehistoric times; corroborating evidence about their lives is not available.

---

2   *Historically, a large number of humans have achieved Nirvana, but the twenty-four Tirthankaras are more auspicious because they helped the laypeople in following the righteous path.*

The twenty-third Tirthankara, Parshvanatha, was born in 949 BC. He achieved Nirvana at the age of one hundred in 849 BC. Tirthankara Vardhamaan Mahavira was born in 599 BC, 250 years after Tirthankara Parshvanatha.

Illustration 2
Names and Cognizances of the Twenty-four Tirthankaras

Names		Cognizances		
Tradition	Digambara Tradition	Shvetambara Tradition	Trees
1. Rishabhanatha or Adinatha	(bull)	(bull)	Banyan tree
2. Ajitanatha	(elephant)	(elephant)	Devil's tree
3. Sambhavanatha	(horse)	(horse)	Sal tree
4. Abhinandana	(monkey)	(monkey)	Charoli tree
5. Sumatinatha	(koka bird)	(krauncha bird)	Callicarpa macrophylla
6. Padmaprabha	(red lotus)	(red lotus)	Banyan tree
7. Suparshvanatha	(nandyavarta symbol)	(swastika)	Albizzia lebbeck
8. Chandraprabha	(crescent)	(crescent)	Alexundrian laurel
9. Pushpadanta or Suvidhinatha	(crocodile)	(crocodile)	Wood apple
10. Shitalanatha	(swastika)	(shrivatsa symbol)	Ficus lacor
11. Shreyamsanatha	(rhinoceros)	(rhinoceros)	Saraca indica
12. Vasupujya	(buffalo)	(buffalo)	Symplocos racemosa roxb
13. Vimalanatha	(boar)	(boar)	Blackberry
14. Anantanatha	(porcupine)	(falcon)	Saraca indica
15. Dharmanatha	(vajra symbol)	(vajra symbol)	Bulca monosperma
16. Shantinatha	(antelope)	(antelope)	Celdrus deodara
17. Kunthunatha	(goat)	(goat)	Symplocos racemosa
18. Aranatha	(tagara blossom)	(nandyavarta symbol)	Mangifera indica
19. Mallinatha	(water-jar)	(water-jar)	Saraca indica
20. Munisuvrata	(tortoise)	(tortoise)	Michelia champea
21. Naminatha	(blue lotus)	(blue lotus)	Minusops elengii
22. Neminatha or Aristanemi	(conch)	(conch)	Goat willow
23. Parshvanatha	(serpent)	(serpent)	Fire flame bush
24. Mahavira	(lion)	(lion)	Sal tree

Tirthankara Mahavira was a contemporary of Gautam Buddha, although somewhat older. Today most available knowledge of Jainism begins with his time, and for this reason many Western scholars mistakenly consider him to be the founder of Jainism.

Tirthankara Mahavira was born in a town called Kundalpur, in a princely state of Vaishali in the state of Bihar in eastern India. When he was thirty years old, he renounced his household and became an ascetic. After twelve years of severe asceticism, at the age of forty-two he attained omniscience. Thereafter, he reinstated the religious system of the Jain devotees. In other words, he consolidated the basic Jain teachings of peace, harmony, and renunciation taught two centuries earlier by Tirthankara Parshvanatha and for thousands of years previously by the other twenty-two Tirthankaras. Tirthankara Mahavira threw new light on the perennial quest of the soul with the truth and discipline of nonviolence. He attained Nirvana in 527 BC, at the age of seventy-two. At the time of his death, the Jain community of adherents consisted of 14,000 monks, led by his chief interpreter and head of the order, Gautam Swami; 36,000 nuns, led by Chandana, the chief nun; and 100,000 *shraavks* and 300,000 *shraavikas* (male and female householders who had assumed the rules of living appropriate to a Jain). The immediate successors to Tirthankara Mahavira were his two interpreters, Gautam Swami and Sudharm, and the latter's disciple, Jambu.

Jain Tirthankaras, the enlightened ones who reformed and reinstated the religious order, recognized that conflicts could be avoided if the human mind was taught to control itself. They taught that all life forms share a common goal of ultimate happiness and bliss. They also accepted that human beings differ from one another in their opinions, aspirations, and approaches to life. Despite their differences, though, all people should avoid conflicts. A conflict arises when people believe that their own opinions are the only right ones, that they alone have the truth, and that everyone else must be wrong. Such an attitude generates vain pride, prejudice, and, consequently, contempt and conflict. To believe that a single person has the truth and to deny that others may have some elements of truth is wrong belief.

Tirthankaras are not traditionalists or "orthodox." Their mode of thinking is progressive and revolutionary but tolerant. During their individual eras, they gave a constructive orientation to the integral conflicts between religions. They worshipped nonviolence, equanimity, and tolerance through wholesome thought processes. Through the liberal medium of relativism or multiplicity of viewpoints, they not only made a concerted effort to establish harmony among different religious groups but also uprooted blind faith and orthodox rituals. They were born as humans and achieved godhood in their lifetimes. Thus they exemplify the path to liberation for all. By following the message of Tirthankaras, all living beings can become the creators of their own destiny and attain godhood through their own efforts. This reality is simple and, although hard to achieve, it is attainable.

Jainism is not a proselytizing religion. It does not postulate a leader and its followers worship no deity in expectation of any kind of favors, although image worship was introduced some years after Tirthankara Mahavira's Nirvana. Since Jainism does not believe in a creator-god, there is no worship of godhead in Jain philosophy. To Jains, the images of Tirthankaras remind them of the basic principles of the Jain religion, and they worship them in order to have pure thoughts and as reminders of their ultimate goal of purifying their souls.

Jainism is the only religion that has no concept of god, and yet it is not atheistic. How can that be? In a very telling sense, the Jains have replaced the notion of god with their own nature of things. Jains are accountable to nature and thus to themselves, to their families, their community, and to the vast menagerie of life forms which cohabit this planet with them. Jainism's accessible genius is the total embrace of the earth—so ancient, and yet so contemporary.

Chapter Five

The Basic Principles of Jainism

All things breathing, all things existing, all things
living, all beings whatever should not be slain or treated
with violence, nor insulted, nor tortured, nor driven away.

There are five basic principles of Jainism which every Jain is expected to follow. These are nonviolence; interdependence; manifold aspects; equanimity; and compassion, empathy, and charity.

Nonviolence

A basic tenet of Jainism is nonviolence (*ahimsa*). According to Jains, nonviolence is the supreme religion. They teach and practice ahimsa not only toward human beings but also toward all of nature. It is an unequivocal teaching that is at once ancient and contemporary: Do not injure, abuse, oppress, enslave, insult, torment, torture, or kill any creature or living being.

The teaching of nonviolence refers not only to wars and visible physical acts of violence but also to violence in the hearts and minds of human beings and to a lack of concern and compassion for their fellows and for the natural world. Furthermore, violence is not simply defined by actual harm, for sometimes this is unintentional. It is the intention to harm, the absence of compassion, that makes action violent. Without violent thoughts there could be no violent actions. Of all the religions of the world, Jainism embraces the principle of nonviolence as its central doctrine to the highest degree.

Nonviolence implies reaching out to others while transcending the barriers of caste, creed, religion, sex, faction, and even species. It is an independent state of consciousness. Our physical, emotional, and intellectual states of being limit and confine us; they choke us, degrade us, and make us unhappy. Nonviolence offers the absence of fetters and chains.

Removing ignorance is the first step toward building a world movement for nonviolence. True knowledge consists of self-understanding and self-control. Nonviolence is the highest form of knowledge since it harmonizes one's relations with others. Ahimsa, like Nirvana (*Moksha*), is freedom from the endless drama of opposites; pleasure-pain, happiness-sorrow, attraction-aversion, love-hate, gain-loss, success-failure, wealth-poverty, fear-courage, strength-weakness, victory-defeat, praise-denigration, honor-insult, conflict-harmony, gentleness-aggression, virtue-vice, good-evil, and freedom-bondage.

Nonviolence is freedom from the past, from history, from memory. It is freedom from everything that suffocates, chokes, distresses, and disturbs. Therefore, whatever can be subdued by its opposite is not free; whatever is not free cannot be nonviolent; persons cannot be sensitive to others' plight if they remain prisoners of the human drama being played out by these opposites.

How is this perfect state, where peace and universal love exist, obtained? Desire and its satisfaction cannot be the foundation of relationships with oneself and others. In relation to oneself, desire will only result in restlessness, anxiety about achieving satisfaction, and then worry about retaining what one has. The individual will reach a point where it becomes impossible for him or her to enjoy what was desired and obtained. In relation to others, the other becomes a means of satisfaction, an object to be grasped, retained, and then manipulated. This is why Jainism places such great emphasis on nonpossession. But this nonpossession does not concern only objects, it refers also to desires and control of the lower senses.

It is fashionable in the West to think of nonviolence as a powerless tool, but this is a misunderstanding. Nonviolence is a way of life and a theory of an ideal society. One who believes in and practices nonviolence resists and counters violence by being uninfluenced by it. Nonviolence absorbs the recurrence of violence. It is an expansive, all-embracing love and concern for all living and nonliving beings. Remorse and bitterness are not part of the agenda of nonviolence.

Who are better candidates for understanding the language of love and concern than the youth of today? If nonviolence is to become a world movement, young people will have to assume the leadership of this movement. They have shown tremendous initiative in taking up the cause of environmental protection, furthering peace, and rising above the narrow confines of nationality, ethnicity, and parochialism. Today's youth are global citizens. They understand the only language that is universal: love. And love is possible only through nonviolence.

Legend has it that Alexander the Great abandoned all future conquests across Asia, when in 325 BC he happened to meet naked Jain monks in the Indian village of Taxila.

Their sermon on nonviolence made such an impact on Alexander that he decided to return to Greece. He lost his desire for violent encounters.

It has been asked of Jains that, if all vegetables, grains, and fruits have life, how can one be vegetarian simply by avoiding meat? Jains divide living entities into five categories depending on the number of senses. Thus, there are one-sensed entities (having the sense of touch); two-sensed entities with the sense of touch and taste (for example, worms and leeches); three-sensed entities with touch, taste, and smell such as moths, ants, and lice; four-sensed entities, and five-sensed entities. Vegetables and fruits are one-sensed entities. Jains are expected to consume only one-sensed entities in moderation to sustain life. Even so, vegetables like potatoes or onions or garlic, which grow under the soil and hence may endanger two-sensed entities which live underground, should not be consumed.

Interdependence

Jainism recognizes the fundamental phenomenon of symbiosis or mutual dependence, which forms the basis of the modern-day science of ecology. All life, Jains preach, is bound together by mutual support and interdependence. All aspects of nature belong together and are bound in a physical as well as a metaphysical relationship. Jainism views life as a gift of togetherness, accommodation, and assistance in a universe teeming with interdependent constituents.

Manifold Aspects

The concept of universal interdependence underpins the Jain doctrine of manifold aspects or *Anekantvad*. How can a person be sensitive to other people and their pain? The Jain philosophy of manifold aspects answers this by arguing that there are no theories or theorems or formulas that are capable of describing reality in absolute terms. Nirvana lies in right perception or faith, right knowledge, and right conduct. Simply put, a person should adopt the perspective that one's way is not the final one, one's version is not the only version, and one's truth is not the ultimate truth. There are many ways, several versions, and diverse paths to reach the truth. Each in its own right is legitimate. The world is a multifaceted, ever-changing reality with an infinite number of viewpoints, depending on the time, place, nature, and state of the one who is the viewer and of that which is viewed.

Consider the story of the blind men eager to know an elephant. Each of them put his hands on the different parts of the massive body. The man who searched the elephant's round belly concluded that the animal was something like a round earthen pot; the one who slid his hands down the legs declared that the elephant was pillar-like; while another, who put his hands on the trunk protested that the animal could only be something vertically suspended— long and flexible; and so forth. A man blessed with eyes who watched this, brought the controversy to an end by revealing that an elephant is the sum total of all these different views.

Said differently, the doctrine of manifold aspects states that truth is relative. What is true from one point of view may be questioned from another. Absolute truth cannot be grasped from any single viewpoint. Absolute truth is the sum of all the different viewpoints that make up the universe. Thus, Jainism does not look on the universe from an anthropocentric, ethnocentric, or egocentric viewpoint. It takes into account the viewpoints of other species, other communities and nations, and other human beings.

Equanimity

Jainism demands the avoidance of dogmatic, intolerant, inflexible, aggressive, harmful, and unilateral attitudes toward the world. It inspires personal equanimity toward both animate beings and inanimate substances and objects. It encourages the attitudes of give and take and of "live and let live." Jainism offers a pragmatic peace plan based not on the domination of nature, nations, or other people but on equanimity of mind devoted to the preservation of the balance of the universe.

Compassion, Empathy, and Charity

Jains should affirm prayerfully and sincerely that their hearts are filled with forgiveness for all living beings, that they seek and receive the forgiveness of all beings, that they crave the friendship of all beings, that all beings give them their friendship, and that they have not the slightest feeling of alienation or enmity in their heart for anyone or anything. They also should pray that forgiveness and friendliness reign throughout the world and that all living beings cherish one another.

Chapter Six

The Two Major Groups of Jains

Knowledge of numerous scripture is of no use to a person who has no character. Can thousands of burning lamps give light to a blind person?

Jains presented themselves as one community until 327 BC, that is, two hundred years after Tirthankara Mahavira's Nirvana. According to one account, about that time, a council of monks met to collect the Jain scriptures that were scattered in various recessions (slightly different versions) as a result of oral transmission. A major split in the council occurred because of a difference of opinions among the monks. An important point of controversy pertained to what monks should wear. One group insisted that monks should not wear any clothes, whereas the other group maintained that monks could wear clothes, believing that such essential items as clothes do not constitute material goods. Eventually, toward the beginning of the Christian era, this dispute resulted in the formation of two main groups of Jain monks. Digambaras, which literally means "sky-clad," and Shvetambaras, which means "clad in white." The lay community also divided accordingly and came to be known as Digambaras or Shvetambaras. Both groups have spread throughout India. They have lived side by side for centuries with very little interaction, although they both subscribe to the same basic principles of Jainism.

A common practice of both groups has been idol worship. They have built temples where idols of different Tirthankaras are placed. In Shvetambara temples, the idols are ornamented and decorated, while in Digambara temples the idols are naked. About AD 1450, several Shvetambara monks formed a new group called the Reformist Monks, which came to be known as the Sthaanakavaasis (meaning "dwellers in halls"). They distinguished themselves from the two earlier groups that worshipped in temples. They maintained that the worship of images of the Tirthankaras was not permitted in the scriptures so instead of building temples, members of this group built *sthaanaks* (prayer halls) where monks and laypeople could meditate. The Sthaanakavaasis introduced strict rules of residence for the monks, and the monks began to use a piece of cloth against the mouth (*muhapatti*) to minimize the violence against small organisms. Over time, several subgroups of Sthaanakavaasis have emerged, such as Terapanthi, Byistolla and others.

Today, three types of Jains can be identified: Digambara, Shvetambara, and Sthaanakavaasi (some scholars consider Sthaanakavaasi to be a sub-group of Shvetambara). They all believe in the basic Jain philosophy, the theory of Karma, the Jain principles, the code of conduct, and the twenty-four Tirthankaras. What distinguishes one group from another is their method of worshipping and the place where they worship. In addition, there is a fundamental difference in the Shvetambara and Digambara sects regarding the role of women. Digambaras maintain that women can become ascetics but that they cannot attain Nirvana; they must be reborn as men to realize that state. Shvetambaras, however, believe that a woman can become a Tirthankara. In fact, according to the Shvetambara sect Tirthankara Mallinatha, the nineteenth Tirthankara, was a woman, although Digambaras do not accept this.

Although there are some eighteen points of difference between Shvetambaris and Digambaris, the issue of nudity was an apparent source of scrutiny between the two groups. Shvetambara monks never go naked, while Digambari monks do.

Chapter Seven

Jain Gods

Jainism teaches us to live harmoniously and it shows how it is possible to do so in a world of contradiction and pain.

Many scholars have asked if Jains believe in God. Jains do believe in the existence of god because if this belief is taken out of the religion there is no purpose to praying. The truth is, Jainism gives the pure, scientific, and true definition of God. According to Jains, once the soul is devoid of all Karmas and desires, it becomes God. At this state the fully developed consciousness of a person acquires complete knowledge and becomes blithesome and supreme. Jains do not believe in God as creator or nurturer. According to Jains, a God who is considered a creator or a nurturer would be endowed with desires, and such an entity cannot have attained complete perfection. Until complete perfection is achieved, a soul cannot be considered as that of God.

Jains worship their gods because they reveal the path to salvation and lead the devotees along that path. They adore them because they help laypeople achieve their ultimate goal. Jain gods are pure and free from all spiritual defects. Such freedom is acquired by completely eradicating and destroying all Karmas and desires, by adopting a strenuous path of spiritual discipline or yoga (combined activity of body, speech, and mind), by meditation, and by severe penance. This way all the infirmities (Karmas) associated with the pure spiritual self or soul are destroyed.

After the destruction of all the Karmas, a person achieves omniscience or *Kevelajnana*. Being omniscient, he qualifies to be the leader of humanity or an *Arhant,* as the Jains call such a person. Some Arhants go about the world preaching the spiritual truth that they have achieved. They are interested in the welfare of all humankind, irrespective of caste and race. Every person is entitled to learn truth. Therefore, Jainism permits all people, without consideration of social distinctions, to approach the Arhants for the acquisition of spiritual knowledge.

Jainism believes in a casteless and classless society. Arhants, perfectly pure in themselves, endowed with infinite knowledge, unbounded sympathy, and love for all living beings, are worshipped as the supreme benevolent personage of humankind. The spiritual purity of the Arhants is so sublime and grand that in their presence there is no evil or hatred. A tiger and a lamb move about in their presence without either ferocity or fear.

On leaving the world, all the Arhants achieve Nirvana and become *Siddhas*. Those Siddhas that have served as teachers while they are Arhants are called Tirthankaras. Jains recognize all the Arhants and all the Siddhas as a group and the twenty-four Tirthankaras individually and collectively as their gods. It is difficult to keep track of all the perfect souls (i.e., Arhants and Siddhas), but we do know the twenty-four Tirthankaras. (According to some Jain authorities, there are currently no Arhants. Other students of Jainism claim that no one knows this, because

Arhants might be living in isolated places.) Shvetambaras and Digambaras position the idols of different Tirthankaras in the temples and offer their prayers in front of them. They worship all the Arhants and Siddhas as a group. The Sthaanakavaasis remember the Tirthankaras as well as the Arhants and Siddhas in their prayer halls, but they do not pray in front of idols.

Chapter Eight

Jain Prayers

Reverence of all life is the core of Jainism, and it articulates how it is possible to do so through adopting the path of nonviolence.

Prayers are an essential part of Jains' lives and every important occasion begins with a prayer. Praying is common in the morning as well as before retiring for the night.

There are a number of reasons why we pray. We pray because praying provides mental peace by diverting attention from routine life, reminds us of the virtues of the great souls, has a sobering effect on our ego, and uplifts our spirits and provides a moral boost in the midst of problems and difficulties.

The most important Jain prayer is called the *Namokar Mantra* or Reverence Recitation or Obeisance Prayer. A *mantra* is a prayer with spiritual powers, and the word *Namo* means "Bowing, I submit myself to you."

The Namokar Mantra is a unique prayer. In this prayer believers do not ask for material favors but meditate on the virtues they should be developing. Their aim is to uplift their own souls through recitation of the noble qualities of the Tirthankaras, monks, and sages. Jains do not pray to any one specific entity, but they salute the qualities of each and every great soul (i.e., all the Arhants, Siddhas, and the twenty-four Tirthankaras as well as other teachers). Altogether there are five lines in the prayer for bowing to five entities, who are sometimes called *Panch Parameshthi* (the five supreme beings). The last four lines are added to the prayer to clarify the significance of the first five. The following is the Hindi version of the *Namokar Mantra* with an English translation. The spiritual relevance of the mantra is explained after each section.

In addition, there are five other prayers that Jains recite: Universal Forgiveness and Friendship Prayer; Universal Peace Prayer; Bhaktamar Stotra; Aspirational Prayer; and Thanksgiving Prayer.

Namokar Mantra (Reverence Recitation or Obeisance Prayer)

NAMO ARAHANTANAM

We revere the supreme human beings because they achieve absolute truth by conquering their inner enemies such as jealousy, greed, anger, egotism, and pride and devote their lives for the uplift of life on earth.

Arithantanam: *Ari* means enemy, and *hant* means destroyer. So the word Arhant means destroyer of the enemy. Which enemy? We may have problems with many people we encounter as friends, acquaintances, neighbors, or in business dealings. Over time, the problems are forgotten or overcome and we do not call them enemy forever. But if, as an example, a tendency of jealousy developed within us and we could not overcome it, it would last forever. Thus, the tendency of jealousy is a real enemy. Winning over jealousy is far more difficult than winning over people. Thinking about those who do not get jealous helps us overcome our own jealousy, so we respect the ones who do not get jealous. It is the same way with anger, greed, pride, and egotism. If our car battery is weak, we jump start it with a stronger battery. Similarly, when we are spiritually weak, we seek connection to those who are strong. We establish such a connection when we recite "Namo Arahantanam."

NAMO SIDDHANAM

We revere the supreme beings or liberated ones because they are souls having absolute perception, knowledge and bliss.

Siddhanam: *Siddha* means an accomplished one who has successfully reached the goal. We all have different goals at different times. Some goals are easier to attain than others. The most difficult goal is to get rid of all Karmas, both good and bad. The fruit of accomplishing this goal is achieving Moksha or Nirvana, where there is happiness forever. All souls in Moksha are liberated from the cycles of incarnations: births, deaths, and rebirths. Until this liberation comes, we have to go through a long cycle of reincarnations in different forms. These different forms of life are animals, insects, vegetables, amoebas, and so on. Among all these, life as a human being is most rare; only human life can achieve Moksha, and therefore it is the most important one. The chain of incarnations is known as life-ocean and Moksha is the shore. In Moksha there is no death, no sickness, no poverty, no insults, and none of the fears we experience in this world. In Moksha there is limitless knowledge, power, peace, and bliss. In order to reach this goal of Moksha, we pay our homage to those who have achieved it. So we bow to them when we recite "Namo Siddhanam."

NAMO AYIRIYANAM

We revere the sages [religious authorities] *who preach, because they master the principles of religion* (i.e., experience self-realization of their souls through self-control, self-sacrifice, character, and penance).

NAMO UVAJJHAYANAM

We revere the sages [religious teachers] *who study because they engage in enhancing their knowledge of matter and soul, and teach the importance of the spiritual over material wealth.*

NAMO LOYE SAVVA SAHUNAM

We revere all sages [ascetics] *because they devote their lives to selfless pursuit of the enlightenment of all, and thus inspire us to live virtuous lives.*

Ayiriya, Uvajjhaya, Sahu: These are all gurus (priests) at different levels who live in society. In this prayer, they are identified in three classes: *Acharya, Upadhyay,* and *Sadhu.* The lowest level is the *Sadhu.* The Sadhu renounces family life, leaving parents, brothers, sisters, husband or wife, children, and all other relatives, and giving away home, money, jewelry, and all wealth. A Sadhu takes five vows: (a) nonviolence, (b) truth, (c) nonstealing, (d) celibacy, and (e) nonpossession for the rest of this life. Such a person spends the time learning scriptures and meditating. Meditation is a state in which the mind and body are completely focused on *Atma* (the Hindi word for soul).

After learning a certain number of scriptures, a Sadhu may rise to become an *Upadhyay.* Just as not all students become teachers, not all Sadhus become Upadhyays. Every group of Sadhus and Upadhyays has a leader who is called an *Acharya*. Acharyas devote themselves to the simplest life humanly possible, completely following the vows mentioned above. According to knowledgeable sources, currently, there are over five thousand Acharya, Upadhyay, and Sadhu living. Among them, about 70 are Digambari ascetics.

In the third, fourth, and fifth lines of the prayer, we bow to all the Acharyas, Upadhyays, and Sadhus. They keep the message of the Tirthankaras alive.

ESO PANCH NAMOKKARO

The recitation of reverence to the above five benedictors

SAVVA PAVAPPANASANO

is capable of destroying all the sins.

MANGALANANCH SAVVESIM

Among all the auspicious prayers

PADAMAM HAVAI MANGALAM

this one is the foremost.

We should revere the above five benedictors with a determination to follow in their footsteps and make our lives meaningful.

In sum, the sacred Jain prayer, the Namokar Mantra, reveres the five types of great souls: Arhants (enlightened souls), Siddhas (liberated souls), Acharyas (religious authorities), Upadhyayas (religious teachers), and Sadhus (ascetics). Such reverence is never paid in expectation of worldly favors or grace but instead acts as a personal inspiration to follow the very same path shown by those spiritual exemplars. A layperson moves toward this goal by adopting the five "minor" vows of nonviolence, truth, non-stealing, chastity (relationship only with married spouse), and nonpossession.

It will be noted in hierarchy of the five types of great souls that Siddhas (liberated souls) come first. Becoming a Siddha is the highest aspiration of a Jain. Despite that in Namokar Mantra, we bow to the Arhants (enlightened souls) first. The rationale for this is that the Arhants teach us; Siddhas do not. Besides, becoming an Arhant is extremely difficult. Once a person becomes an Arhant, it is only a matter of time before he becomes a Siddha.

How many times should a Jain recite Namokar Mantra? It could be recited as many as 108 times a day. The number 108 represents the total number of all attributes or qualities of the five great souls. At the minimum, one should recite Namokar Mantra at least three times daily; the number three represents the three jewels of Jainism. Often, devotees recite Namokar Mantra nine times to twenty-one times, which is fine as well.

Universal Forgiveness and Friendship Prayer

After the celebration of Paryushan/Dash Lakshana (see chapter 13), Jains offer the following prayer of forgiveness and friendship by visiting relatives and friends or communicating with them through mail or e-mail.

- I forgive (from the bottom of my heart without any reservation) all living beings (who may have caused me any pain and suffering either in this life or previous lives).
- I beg (again from the bottom of my heart without any reservation) for the forgiveness from all living beings (no matter how small or big) to whom I may have caused pain and suffering in this life or previous lives, knowingly or unknowingly, mentally, verbally, or physically, or if I have asked or encouraged someone else to carry out such activities.
- (Let all creatures know that) I have a friendship with everybody.
- I have no revenge (animosity or enmity) toward anybody.

Universal Peace Prayer

May the entire universe be blessed;
May all beings engage in each other's well being;
May all weakness, sickness, and faults vanish;
May everyone be healthy, peaceful, and blessed everywhere.

Bhaktamar Stotra

The *Bhaktamar Stotra* had been composed by a religious authority, Acharya Manatunga Surisvarji, in praise of the first Tirthankara Rishabhanatha sometime during the 6th and 7th century AD. The Bhaktamar Stotra has forty-eight stanzas. Each stanza is rich in deep devotion and high poetic flight. Further, the stanzas suggest gestures to mediate upon different divine aspects of Tirthankara Rish-bhanatha.

The chanting of the Bhaktamar Stotra creates an intense feeling of devotion toward the Tirthankara, and the silent meditation imbibes the spirit of the Tirthankara, which is none other than one's Real Self. As an example, consider meditation on stanzas thirty-four to forty-three, which emphasize fearlessness. It is said that a person need not be afraid of the following eight enemies if he or she recites the hymns. These enemies are (1) Mad Elephant-Ego; (2) Lion-Power; (3) Fire- Anger; (4) Serpent-Vengeance; (5) War-Death; (6) Stormy Sea-Evil Desires; (7) Dropsy-Disease; (8) Bondage-Body Idea.

Legend has it that during Acharya Manatunga Surisvarji's time there were two scholars of great repute—Pandit Mayura and Pandit Bana. They influenced the rulers with their mantric and tantric power and were duly rewarded. The Jain Acharyas and Sadhus were accused of lacking such powers and were considered unfit; therefore, they were banished from the kingdom.

Acharya Manatunga Surisvarji preached Jain religion at that time. He was summoned and asked by the king to prove the greatness of Jina. He answered that our Jina free from love and hatred does not perform any miracles. The king got upset and ordered that the Acharya be fettered in forty-eight chains and be stationed behind the Jain temple. Subsequently, the Acharya composed and began singing the Bhaktamar Stotra, and with every new composition the fetters got cut off one by one. When the entire stotra was completed, the temple had turned 180 degrees to face the Acharya.

This legend contains a profound contemporary message for today's men and women. The iron fetters or chains are nothing but chains of disturbing human emotions such as anger, greed, lust, desire, and fear, which have tied down the modern human. He or she still holds, deep down inside, the power of spiritual awakening and freedom. The turning of the entire temple reflects the power of deep devotion.

The forty-eight *Bhaktamar* stanzas are listed in Appendix B at the end.

Aspirational Prayer

(1 & 2) May my mind be devotedly absorbed in Him who has vanquished affection and hatred, who has found out the reality of all that exists, who has explained the path of liberation to all living beings without any expectation (of worship from them). You may call him Buddha, Vira, Jina, Hari, Hara, Brahma, or Self-controlled.

(3 & 4) Those who have no desire for sense-pleasures, who are rich in equanimity, who are constantly engaged in bringing about the good for themselves and for others, who suffer the severe asceticism of renouncing all selfish interests, without any regret—such learned ascetics remove the multitude of troubles of the world.

(5) May I ever have their good company; may I ever have them in my mind; may my heart be always engrossed in following their rules of conduct.

(6) May I never cause an injury to any living being; may I never speak a lie; may I never be tempted towards the

wife or husband or property of another; may I ever remain contented.

(7) May I never entertain an idea of egotism; may I never be angry with anybody; may I never feel jealous on seeing the prosperity of other people.

(8) May I always act in a simple and straightforward manner; may I always, so far as it lies in my power, be willing to help others.

(9) May I ever have a friendly regard for all living beings in the world; and may the stream of compassion always flow from my heart towards distressed and afflicted persons.

(10) May I never be wrathful towards wicked and cruel persons and those fond of evil ways. May I be tolerant towards them; may I be so disposed.

(11) May my heart be overflowing with love at the sight of persons possessed of good qualities; may my mind feel happy by serving them so far as lies in my power.

(12) May I never be ungrateful; may I never have malice in my heart. May I ever appreciate the good qualities of other persons; may I never look at their faults.

(13 & 14) May my steps never slip from the path of rectitude, whether I be considered good or bad by other persons, whether wealth comes to me or goes away from me, whether I may live for hundreds of years or meet death this day, whether I am terrified in any manner or tempted in any way.

(15 & 16) May my mind never be puffed up with joy; may it never be distressed in trouble; may it never be afraid of a mountain, a river, a cremation ground, or a terrible forest. May it always remain unshaken and firm, may it become stronger; may it exhibit endurance on occasions of deprivation of good things, and occurrence of evil happenings.

(17) May all living beings in the world be happy; may nobody ever feel distressed; may everybody renounce enmity, sin, pride, and always sing fresh songs of joy.

(18) May there be religious talk in every home; may evil deeds become impossible; may everybody improve his knowledge and conduct, and enjoy the fruit of being born a human being.

(19) May calamity and terror never spread in the world; may there be rains at the proper time; may the leaders be righteous, and may they administer justice to all.

(20) May disease and pestilence never spread; may all live peacefully; may the religion of Ahimsa pervade the world, and bring about universal good.

(21) May there be love amongst all; may ignorance keep away at distance; may nobody utter an unkind, bitter, or harsh word.

(22) May every brave youth be heartily engaged in the progress of righteousness; may he realize the reality of things and suffer with pleasure every trouble and every misfortune.

Thanksgiving Prayer[3]

Today we give thanks for this vegetarian meal and the people who have labored to harvest and prepare this meal for us. We give thanks for the many lives that have contributed to our lives. We also ask for forgiveness from living beings that we have harmed, intentionally or unintentionally.

We are grateful for our health and the opportunity to eat with others on this day. We aspire, with compassionate hearts, to use the energy that we gain from this meal and our friends to contribute to the peace and happiness of all living beings.

We pray that all the people of the world will avoid inflicting harm on animals and fellow human beings and practice nonviolence and compassion. We express our sorrow at the suffering of all the turkeys and other animals that have died. May peace and compassion grow in ourselves and extend to all around us.

---

3   The original draft of this prayer was prepared by Pravin K. Shah and was edited by Jaina Education Committee.

Chapter Nine

The Jain Concept of Time

*Happiness is an attribute of the soul and one
has to attain it from the soul itself.*

Jains assume that the universe, with all its components, is
without a beginning or an end, being everlasting and eternal. Time moves cyclically, as a wheel moves. As the cycle
ascends, humankind prospers, and happiness and life span
increase; and as the cycle descends, prosperity, happiness,
and life span decrease.

In each circle, that is, from the descending to the as-
cending stage, there are four periods, which are called
Dwaapar, Kaliyug, Treta, and *Satayug.* Each period consists
of three eras. Ascendance in the left direction is called *Utsarpini* while in the right direction it is known as *Avasarpini.*
Currently, we are in the first era of the Kaliyug period. Next,
we will be heading in the Utsarpini direction to ascend in
the Treta period. The Jain concept of time is depicted in
illustration 3.

Illustration 3
The Time Cycle in Jainism

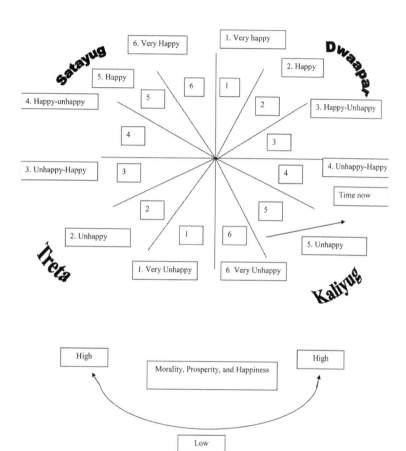

Chapter Ten

The Three Jewels of Jainism

Conquer anger by forgiveness, pride by humility, deceit by straight forwardness and greed by contentment.

Jainism stresses that ultimate happiness can be achieved only by shedding all the Karmas, thus breaking the cycle of birth and rebirth. In other words, the ultimate goal is the achievement of Nirvana. To realize this goal, one should concentrate on the three jewels of Jainism: *rational perception* or *belief, rational knowledge,* and *rational conduct.*

According to Jainism, rationalism is essential for spiritual development. Rationalism helps minimize the negative influence of Karmas on a person's life and also creates a proper frame of mind.

The First Jewel: Rational Perception or Rational Belief or Rational Faith

Rational perception is the belief in the aspects of reality, that is, in only what seems reasonable according to one's observation, study, and experience. The emphasis here is on what is logical and appeals to common sense. We should not accept anything simply because it is written in a book or is preached by an individual. We should not believe in dogma, hearsay, or superstition. As an example, in the early post-Vedic Age in India, people zealously competed in giving hyperbolic descriptions of deities. This exercise resulted in the human image of greatness being enshrouded in superhuman miracles. But such a perspective is not realistic. Therefore, Jainism rejects it. Rational perception has three aspects: *belief in the auspicious, freedom from three kinds of superstitions,* and *cultivation of life through eight-fold virtues.*

A. <u>Belief in the auspicious</u>
   a. supreme human beings (Arhants)
   b. teachings from scriptures
   c. monks, who fully practice the scriptures' teachings

B. <u>Freedom from superstitions</u>
   a. common misconceptions
   b. deity-related misconceptions
   c. guru-related misconceptions

C. <u>Cultivation through virtues</u>
   a. absence of suspicion
   b. absence of desire
   c. absence of revulsion
   d. absence of indiscreetness
   e. absence of criticism
   f. support of the beguiled
   g. admiration of the virtuous
   h. advancement of the virtuous path

The Second Jewel: Rational Knowledge

Rational knowledge refers to knowledge that reveals the true nature of a thing, exactly as it is, with certainty. It should neither be insufficient nor exaggerated. Rational knowledge provides the full comprehension of the real nature of soul and non-soul (i.e., matter) without doubt, perversity, and vagueness.

Five kinds of knowledge can be distinguished:

a. <u>Sense-knowledge</u>: It is knowledge of the self and non-self acquired by means of any of the five senses and the mind.
b. <u>Scriptural-knowledge</u>: It is derived from the reading or hearing of scriptures.
c. <u>Clairvoyant-knowledge</u>: It is the knowledge of things in distant time or place. It can be acquired by saints who have attained purity of thought and developed their mental capacity through austerities.
d. <u>Mental-knowledge</u>: It is the direct knowledge of another's mental activity, that is, knowledge about thoughts and feelings of others. It can be acquired by those who have gained self-mastery.
e. <u>Perfect-knowledge or Omniscience:</u> It is full or perfect knowledge without the limitations of time and space, which is the soul's characteristic in its pure and indefinable condition. It draws on the Tirthankaras and perfect souls.

Acquisition of rational knowledge has the following requirements:

a. <u>Correct use of words:</u> It means that reading, writing, and pronouncing of every letter and word should be done correctly.
b. <u>Understanding meaning:</u> It means that reading should be directed towards understanding the

meaning and full significance of words, phrases, and the text. In other words, reading without understanding the meaning serves no purpose.

c. <u>Combination of correct use and meaning</u>: It stresses that both reading and understanding of the meaning are essential as together they complete the process.

d. <u>Observance of regularity and propriety of time</u>: It means that improper and unsuitable occasions should be avoided. Again, the time chosen for study must be peaceful and free from disturbance due to worries and anxieties.

e. <u>Reverent attitude</u>: It means that humility and respect towards the scriptures should be cultivated to develop devotion to learning.

f. <u>Propriety</u>: While studying, one may come across difficult expressions and inexplicable ideas. In such cases one should not draw hasty conclusions which might lead to improper behavior.

g. <u>Zeal</u>: Zeal in the mastery of the subject under study is also essential to sustain interest and continuity.

h. <u>Non-concealment of knowledge and its sources</u>: It is suggested that one must keep an open mind and attitude so that narrow considerations do not shut one out from fullness of knowledge.

In summary, rational knowledge is knowledge or information obtained through study of the scriptures, accompanied by careful thinking and analysis. Rational knowledge is derived through two sources: external and internal. *External knowledge* is knowledge acquired through the senses and knowledge acquired through signs, symbols, letters, and words. *Internal knowledge* is extraordinary knowledge such as knowledge of objects and events perceived in distant places, times, or both; mental knowledge such as telepathy or the ability to communicate with others mentally; and absolute knowledge.

The Third Jewel: Rational Conduct

After rational belief and rational knowledge, the third but the most important path to the goal of Moksha, or salvation, is rational conduct. In Jainism, the utmost importance is attached to rational conduct because rational belief and rational knowledge equip the individual with freedom from delusion only providing him with true knowledge of the fundamental principles. These principles prepare the person to seek rational conduct which ultimately leads to salvation. That is why conduct which is inconsistent with right belief and knowledge is considered wrong conduct or misconduct. Thus, conduct becomes perfect only when it is in tune with rational belief and rational knowledge.

In accordance with Jain philosophy, rational conduct presupposes the presence of rational knowledge, which presupposes the existence of rational belief. Therefore, the Jain scriptures have enjoined the persons who have secured rational belief and rational knowledge to observe the rules of rational conduct, as the destruction of karmic matter associated with the soul can be accomplished only through the practice of rational conduct.

Rational conduct entails a proper lifestyle that helps a person minimize physical and mental violence to self and other living beings. This involves living in harmony with fellow beings and with nature.

There are five major aspects of the Jain's code of conduct: They are: (a) the *five vows of nonviolence, truth, non-stealing, celibacy* (or *chastity*), and *non-possessiveness*; (b) *kindness to animals*; (c) *vegetarianism*; (d) *self-restraint and the avoidance of waste*; and (e) *charity*. In addition, Jains should observe seven *supplementary vows*.

The Jain's code of conduct is in many respects similar to the ethical code preached by other religions. Jainism, however, emphasizes that one's conduct cannot be rational without rational perception or rational belief and rational knowledge.

It may be asked how, on the basis of our own understanding and experience, we can determine what proper conduct is. The answer is simple: We know that passions such as anger and greed make us unhappy. They destroy our peace of mind. We don't enjoy being hurt physically. We do not like to have our feelings hurt and we feel awful when we hurt someone else's feelings. Thoughts of violence and revenge upset us. If we have an undue attachment to a material good, we become unhappy when it is lost or damaged. In contrast, if we learn to be content with what we have, we enjoy real happiness. Our rational conduct should be guided by such observations and experiences.

Underlying the Jain code of conduct is the emphatic assertion of individual responsibility for one and all. Indeed, the entire universe is the forum of one's own conscience.

The code is profoundly ecological in its secular thrust and its practical consequences.

A. <u>The Five Vows</u>
   a. To practice nonviolence in thought, word, and deed;
   b. To seek and speak the truth;
   c. To behave honestly and to take nothing by force or theft;
   d. To practice restraint and chastity in thought, word, and deed (i.e., honest marital relationship);
   e. To practice non-acquisitiveness or non-possessiveness.

The vow of nonviolence is the first and pivotal vow. The other vows may be viewed as aspects of nonviolence, which together form an integrated code of conduct in the individual's quest for equanimity. The vows are undertaken at an austere and exacting level by monks and nuns and are then called *great vows*. They are undertaken at a more moderate and flexible level by householders and are called the *basic vows*.

<u>Nonviolence</u>: Nonviolence (ahimsa) is the foundation of the Jain outlook on life. The Jain religion teaches that all life is sacred. Every living being has a unique place in the scheme of the universe.

Violence may be defined as obstruction of the life processes of oneself and of others through a lack of conscientiousness. All living beings have to interact with their environment, which includes other living beings, such as plants and animals. Thus, violence in life is unavoidable to a certain extent, but Jains should avoid intentional violence of any kind. Ancient Jain thinkers classified living beings on the basis of the complexity of their life processes. The life processes of plants are simple while those of animals are highly developed. The higher the form of life, the greater the violence involved in hurting or killing it. The Jain practice of vegetarianism is based on this concept because less violence is committed in procuring and processing vegetarian foods. Even the violence toward plant life should be kept to a minimum. Further, when someone commits physical and mental violence toward another human being, it leads to undesirable thoughts. The feelings of the people involved are hurt in the process, which produces even more violence.

The Jain concept of nonviolence promotes peace and harmony in society. An atmosphere of kindness surrounds a person of kindly temperament. Jainism firmly holds that life is sacred, irrespective of species, caste, color, creed, or nationality. A resident of New Delhi is as sacred as a resident of New York or London: the person's color, food, and dress are external adjuncts. The practice of nonviolence is both an individual and a collective virtue. This kindly attitude, which requires that our hearts be free from baser impulses such as anger, pride, hypocrisy, greed, envy, and contempt has a positive force and a universal appeal.

Truth: Truthfulness is an important virtue that eliminates suspicion and mistrust among individuals and creates an atmosphere of security in society. We should always speak the truth. We should perform our duties well and to the best of our ability. These are essential aspects of the vows of truth. By practicing the vows of truth, we earn the trust of others. This vow promotes neighborliness and enables us to become a Jain in the true sense of the word.

One's thoughts, words, and acts must all be consistent. Further, they must create an atmosphere of confidence. A reciprocal sense of security must start with one's immediate neighbor and then be gradually diffused in society at large, not just in theory but also in practice. These virtues can lead to coherent social and political groups of worthy citizens who yearn for peaceful coexistence with the well-being of all humanity in view.

Nonstealing: We should abstain from taking anything that does not belong to us. No matter what the circumstances are and how exciting the deed could be, one should never steal anything from another individual. The emotions that might lead you to steal should be controlled. We should take only our fair share and should not indulge in any unfair business practices. We should also minimize what we take from nature. Taking more than our just share is equivalent to stealing from nature.

Celibacy: All men have some yearning for sensual or sexual pleasure. However common this may be, such desires cause unhappiness. Minimizing our needs and gradually eliminating desires are important goals in life.

One of the fundamental principles of Jainism is individual freedom, but our freedom should not infringe on others' rights. It should not lead to problems in our lives and in society. Jains should practice celibacy. Jain monks practice total celibacy while the householders abstain from premarital and extramarital sex and observe partial celibacy. Celibacy maintains purity of body and mind and helps to minimize life's problems. About one-half of teen-agers in the United States refrain from premarital sex, apparently with no mental or physical damage. The other half does not refrain and suffers venereal diseases, unwanted pregnancy, and emotional problems. It requires no genius to know which half is better off.

<u>Non-possessiveness:</u> This is the fifth vow of the Jains. It entails limiting needs and minimizing greed. It helps conserve energy and other natural resources. Its practice can result in social equity and justice. A highly religious person is free from possessiveness in thought, word, and deed. Others practice non-possessiveness to varying degrees depending on their stage of spiritual development.

It is observed that most problems, individual ones as well as collective ones, arise from indulgence in indiscriminate acquisitiveness. People tell lies, cheat, deceive, and use unfair means in the service of greed. Such practices are a form of violence toward self. In the final analysis, the last four vows help us minimize self-directed violence.

Jainism preaches ignoring, as much as possible, the economic distinctions between rich and poor and the social distinctions between high and low. Avoiding these distinctions can be achieved by following the vow of non-possessiveness. The Jain ascetics, according to this vow, own no property of their own. Without possessions, the ascetic depends on the laity or the householders for sustenance. Sustained by society, the ascetic devotes all of his time and energy to promoting the spiritual and cultural development of society as a whole. The laypeople or householders are the mainstay of social organization: they maintain the economic stability of society. It is incumbent on them to see that wealth does not accumulate in a few hands. They must prevent poverty and misery from becoming concentrated. In order to secure such economic harmony, they are expected to follow the main economic principle, one based on the moral idea of setting apart a small portion of their wealth for themselves and using the rest of their possessions for the benefit of society at large.

Such a principle, if strictly followed as a moral ideal, will successfully avoid both an uneven distribution of wealth and the concentration of poverty. It will promote a healthy social organization that considers the welfare of all human beings and society as a whole. Such conduct, when sufficiently promoted and widely practiced, will naturally lead to social development. In such a society there will be no animosity between groups of people, and there will be no possibility of a clash between haves and have-nots. Such a society will create a condition of universal peace and general happiness.

B. Kindness to Animals

Kindness to animals is an extension of the vow of nonviolence. It prohibits all forms of cruelty against animals. Jains condemn as evil the common practice of animal sacrifice to the gods. It is generally forbidden to keep animals in captivity, to whip, mutilate, or overload them or to deprive them of adequate food and drink. The injunction is modified in respect to domestic animals to the extent that they may be roped or even whipped occasionally but always mercifully, with due consideration and without anger.

C. Vegetarianism

Except for allowing themselves a judicious use of one-sensed life in the form of grains, vegetables and fruits, and dairy products such as milk, butter, and cheese, Jains do not consciously take any life for food or sport. As a community they are strict vegetarians, consuming no meat, fish, or eggs. They confine themselves to grains, vegetables and fruits, and milk products. Jains constitute the only major religion in the world that is unconditionally vegetarian. The idea of consuming an animal is nearly as horrifying to the Jains as an act of outright murder.

D. Self-Restraint and the Avoidance of Waste

The Jain laity endeavor to live a life of moderation and restraint and to practice a measure of abstinence and austerity. They must not procreate indiscriminately lest they overburden the world and its resources. Regular periods of fasting for self-purification are encouraged.

In their use of the earth's resources, Jains take their cue from: "the bee sucks honey in the blossoms of a tree without hurting the blossom and strengthens itself." Wants should be reduced, desires curbed, and consumption levels kept within reasonable limits. Using any resource beyond one's needs and misusing any part of nature are considered forms of theft. Indeed, the Jain faith goes one radical step further and declares unequivocally that creating waste and pollution are acts of violence.

E. Charity

Accumulation of possessions and enjoyment for personal ends should be minimized. Making charitable donations and giving generously of one's time for community projects are components of a Jain householder's obligations. That explains why the Jain temples and pilgrimage centers are well endowed and well managed. It is this sense of social obligation, born out of religious teachings, that has led the Jains to establish and maintain innumerable schools, colleges, hospitals, clinics, lodging houses, hostels, orphanages, relief and rehabilitation camps for the handicapped, old, sick, and disadvantaged as well as hospitals for ailing birds and animals. Wealthy individuals are advised to recognize that beyond a certain point their wealth is superfluous and that they should manage the surplus as trustees for social benefit.

Supplementary Vows

The supplementary vows consist of (a) multiplicative vows and (b) disciplinary vows. Together these vows increase the value of the major vows.

The *multiplicative vows* require taking a lifelong vow to limit one's worldly activities to fixed points in all directions: limiting worldly activities to a limited area and abstaining from wanton and sinful activities. The *disciplinary vows* require taking a vow to devote specific time every day to contemplation or meditation for spiritual development, fasting four days a month (i.e., two eighth and two fourteenth days of the month), limiting one's consumption of goods and services, and eating only after feeding the ascetics or, in their absence, the pious householders.

Summary

Most Jains are laypersons who follow the ideal of well-being rather than seeking complete liberation. For them the paths of right perception, right knowledge, and right conduct are followed through modest living, prescribed behavior (e.g., nonviolence), stringent vegetarianism, and acts of rituals and devotion (worship).

In Jain scriptures, thirty-five rules for right conduct are laid out for householders. Discussed above are a few rules directly concerned with the well-being of the family. At the minimum, householders should earn their livelihood honestly and keep their expenses moderate. The family should dress decently and within its means. The household should be kept in a good neighborhood. Marriage should be between two people of similar culture and language with compatible character and taste. (This is not to promote caste, color, or creed prejudices but to avoid disharmony and strife.) Householders should respect their parents and older members of society and should take care of their dependents. These basic principles of Jainism, if correctly understood and earnestly practiced, can make an ideal family and worthy citizens of the world. Illustration 4 summarizes how rational perception, rational knowledge, and rational conduct lead to honest and happy living.

Rational conduct requires that we minimize our passions, anger, pride or ego, inclination toward deception or intrigue, and greed. Furthermore, rational conduct can be total or partial. The above discussion focused on the characteristics of partial rational conduct. Total rational conduct additionally involves *three augmenting vows* (limiting the field of activity, e.g., not eating after sunset; limiting needless activity; and limiting direct or indirect delectations or pleasures), and *four learning vows* (periodically limiting the field of activity; practicing equanimity or calmness; fasting partially or totally; and serving the virtuous).

Illustration 4
The Jewels of Jainism

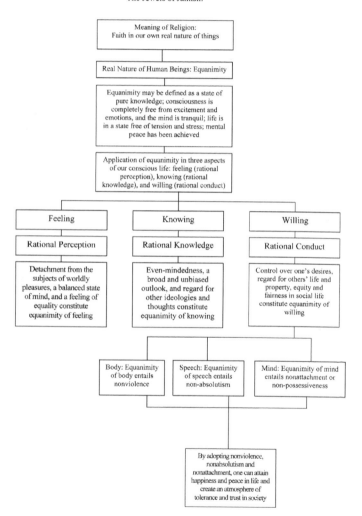

Illustration 4

The Jewels of Jainism

Meaning of Religion:
Faith in our own real nature of things

Real Nature of Human Beings: Equanimity

Equanimity may be defined as a state of pure knowledge; consciousness is completely free from excitement and emotions, and the mind is tranquil; life is in a state free of tension and stress; mental peace has been achieved

Application of equanimity in three aspects of our conscious life: feeling (rational perception), knowing (rational knowledge), and willing (rational conduct)

Feeling	Knowing	Willing
Rational Perception	Rational Knowledge	Rational Conduct
Detachment from the subjects of worldly pleasures, a balanced state of mind, and a feeling of equality constitute equanimity of feeling	Even-mindedness, a broad and unbiased outlook, and regard for other ideologies and thoughts constitute equanimity of knowing	Control over one's desires, regard for others' life and property, equity and fairness in social life constitute equanimity of willing

Body: Equanimity of body entails nonviolence

Speech: Equanimity of speech entails non-absolutism

Mind: Equanimity of mind entails nonattachment or non-possessiveness

By adopting nonviolence, nonabsolutism and nonattachment, one can attain happiness and peace in life and create an atmosphere of tolerance and trust in society

Chapter Eleven

Jaın Symbols

Anger spoils good relations, pride destroys modesty, deceit destroys amity (friendship), greed destroys everything.

Jainism teaches spiritualism and Jains pray to uplift their souls. They don't pray for worldly rewards or comforts, because Jinas are uninvolved in human affairs. Jain image-worship is of a meditational nature. A Jina is seen as an ideal, a certain mode of the soul. Through personification of that idol state in stone, the Jains create a meditative support. (To some extent Buddhists take this position, too; Hindus, however, do expect the deity to return favors in response to their prayers.) When Jains pray they use symbols to take their minds off the material world; a few of these symbols are introduced below.

The Swastika

The Sanskrit word *swast* means well-being and the swastika is the symbol of well-being. Jains use it for meditating on the soul and its place in the universe. It is a tradition to draw the swastika on cloth, paper, metal, wall, etc. at the beginning of many religious and social ceremonies, since it is considered to be a symbol of prosperity and good fortune. The hands of the swastika shown in illustration 5 indicate the four states of existence: human, superhuman (refers to heavenly bodies or celestial gods), subhuman, and hellish. The human state of existence is the highest of all. To become an Arhant and then a Siddha, you have to be a human.

Illustration 5
Jain Swastika

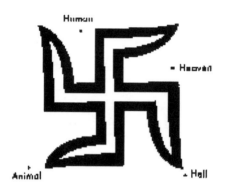

Siddha-chakra

The Siddha-chakra or saint-wheel represents a design of the *Pancha Parmseshti* or five benedictors mentioned in the Namokar Mantra. Cut in stone, cast in metal, or painted on cloth or paper, Jains display Siddha-chakra in their homes and temples or prayer-halls. Its purpose is to remind the laypeople of the five great souls so that they may draw inspiration from them to follow in their footsteps.

Centuries ago, both the Digarmbaras and the Shvetambaras used a lotus of four petals to design their Siddha-chakra. In that design, an Arhant was positioned in the center, a Siddha on the top petal, an Acharya on the right petal, a Upadhya on the left petal, and a Sadhu on the lower petal. Later on, an eight-petaled Siddha-chakra emerged and the Shevetambaras and Digambaras followed a slightly different design. Illustration 6 depicts an eight-petaled Siddha-chakra.

Illustration 6
Explanation of an Eight-petaled Siddha-chakra
(Saint-Wheel)

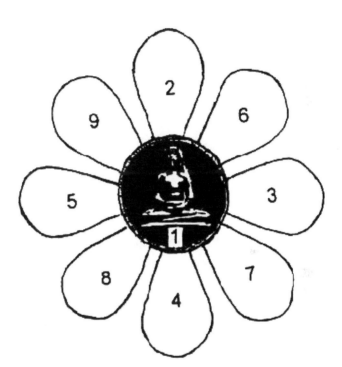

Shvetambara:

1. *Arhat*
2. *Siddha*
3. *Acharya*
4. *Upadhyaya*
5. *Sadhu*
6. *Jnana* (right knowledge)
7. *Darshana* (right faith)

8. *Charitra* (right conduct)
9. *Tapas* (right penance)

Digambara: 1 to 5 as above

6. *Chaitya* (the Jina image)
7. *Chaityalaya* (temple enshrining the Jina)
8. *Dharmachakra* (wheel of law)
9. *Sutras* (represented by a book stand)

The Symbol of the Jain Faith or Emblem of Jain Philosophy

In preparation for the 2,600th anniversary of Tirthankara Mahavira's Nirvana in the mid-1970s, various Jain sects found it desirable to design a common symbol for the Jain religion. The symbol that finally emerged is shown in illustration 7, entitled the Jain Universe. The new composition includes some traditional elements like a swastika and the "Wheel of Law," and a few new features. This symbol is established on Jain principles and beliefs. The POLYGON represents the universe. An ancient Jain SWASTIKA glorifies four innate qualities of the soul: Infinite Knowledge, Perception, Bliss, and Spiritual Strength. It also signifies the four worldly states: human, angel, hell being, and tiryanch (animal, plant, microbe). The THREE POINTS represent the "Three Jewels" of the Jain religion. They are Samyak Darshan (Right Perception), Samyak Gyan (Right Knowledge) and Samyak Charitra (Right Conduct). The LONE POINT above the crescent symbolizes a liberated pure soul. The HAND admonishes man to stop sinning. The WHEEL contains the word AHIMSA, or non-violence. The

Sanskrit edict comes from the scripture Tattvartha Sutra and means, "All life is interdependent."

Illustration 7
The Jain Universe
WE BELIEVE IN AHIMSA – NONVIOLENCE

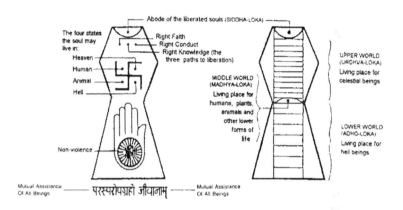

The Eight Objects of Auspiciousness : Asta-Mangalas

Illustration 8 represents the eight objects that Jains in the Shvetambara tradition consider auspicious. They are popular objects of worship in Jain temples. Originally, the eight objects were cut into slabs of stone, but they are now used more often on engraved metal platters and colored paintings on cloth and paper than on stone panels. Previously, each of the eight symbols had its own meaning. (The mirror, for instance, was meant for seeing one's true self.) Today they are looked upon as an "eight-in-one" symbol, the worship of which, when offered in the right frame of mind, is believed to be a good omen. The Asta-Mangala symbol is not rigidly fixed but occurs in various shapes and arrangements.

Illustration 8
The Eight Objects of Auspiciousness:
Asta-Mangalas

Asta-Mangala, the eight objects of auspiciousness in the Shvetambara tradition:

(1) *swastika*;
(2) *shrivatsa*, the mark on the chest of the Jina;
(3) *nadyavarta*, a diagram;
(4) *vardhamanaka*, a powder-flask;
(5) *kalasha*, a full vase, the two eyes representing right knowledge and right faith;
(6) *bhadrasana*, a high seat;
(7) a pair of fish;
(8) a mirror.

The Digambara tradition uses the following set of *Asta-Mangalas* (not illustrated):

(1) *bhrngara*, a type of vessel;
(2) *kalasha*, a full vase;
(3) *darpana*, a mirror;
(4) *camara*, a fly-whisk;
(5) *dhvaja*, a banner;
(6) *vyajana*, a fan;
(7) *chatra*, a parasol; and
(8) *supratistha*, the auspicious seats.

Aum or Om

Aum (or Om) means completeness; it is really a symbolic word representing the infinite, the perfect, and the eternal (see illustration 9). The very sound is complete, representing the wholeness of all things. Aum or Om also

Illustration 9
AUM or OM

represents the Namokar Mantra in Jainism. The word is made up of five letters, a+a+a+u+m = AUM in Sanskrit. The first letter 'A' is for Arihanta, the second letter 'A' is for Ashariri (or without body, Siddha), the third letter 'A' is for Acharya, the fourth letter, 'U' is for Upadhyaya, and the fifth letter, 'M' is for Muni (Sadhu). In this way all five letters constitute AUM or Om. With the help of this mantra, its vibrations and experiences, one can liberate one's soul from the cycle of birth and death.

Hrim

Hrim is a seed mantra, a mystical symbol representing the invisible sound, infinity, and divine energy of the 24 Tirthankaras (see illustration 10). Meditating on Hrim, one experiences the sublimating energy of the Tirthankaras.

Illustration 10
HRIM

Chapter Twelve

Jainism Compared with Other Living Religions

Without faith, there is no knowledge, without knowledge there is no virtuous conduct, without virtues there is no release of Karmas and without release of Karmas there is no emancipation.

Many of the world's religions can be divided into two categories, based on their belief in rebirth. The Hindu, Buddhist, and Jain religions believe in rebirth; Islam, Christianity, and Judaism do not. Jainism has more in common with Hinduism and Buddhism than with Islam, Christianity, and Judaism.

Jainism vs. Hinduism

The Jain religion is an integral part of Indian culture but differs from the Hindu religion in its beliefs regarding incarnation, the creation of the world, and the theory of Karma. Jainism does not accept the theory of an incarnate God who has been born to wash away the sins of people and destroy the sinners, or the notion that the world was created by a deity that is ultimately a guiding or destructive force. The Jain religion believes that every human being is capable of attaining godhood, that is, that any person can become a free liberated soul.

Jains believe that the world has always been here and that it can never be completely destroyed. They accept the principle of time decay—the old gets destroyed—but believe that the basic elements of the world are never destroyed because new, transformed forms come into being. The cycle of change continues forever. Therefore, the need of an extraordinary being or God in control of the world does not exist.

Furthermore, Jainism considers Karmas to be the result of human effort that do not, however, symbolize destiny. Hinduism asserts that we perform Karma but the fruit or reward is dispensed by God. Jainism differs, believing that all enjoy the fruit of their own Karmas, good or bad.

While the Jain religion is fundamentally different from Hinduism, Jain practices have been adapted to Hindu traditions in many ways. For example, although the Jain tradition officially rejects the Hindu *Dharmasastra* (religious code of conduct) and the whole caste system, it has accommodated itself by maintaining social equivalences and surrogate ritual procedures that allow coexistence within the larger Brahmanical–Hindu environment. There is a distinctively Jain style of life, but it adapts itself to the Hindu manner in a great variety of ways, for example, in social customs and behavioral patterns. In fact, in a simple meeting or home visit, one can't distinguish a Hindu from a Jain. Jain art does not differ from Hindu art in form, aesthetic norms, theories of proportions, or formal concepts.

Jains, like Hindus, developed divinities who were associated with laypersons' lives in a benevolent manner. These divinities are guardian spirits who fulfill the mundane wishes of devotees. Here are examples of select divinities:

- *Ambika* (allied with the twenty-second Tirthankara, Neminatha), mother goddess
- *Sarasvati*, goddess of knowledge
- *Sachika* (allied with the first Tirthankara, Adinatha)
- *Lakshmi*, goddess of wealth
- *Chakresvari* (allied with the twenty-fourth Tirthankara, Mahavira)
- *Padmavati* (allied with the twenty-third Tirthankara, Parsvanatha)

In addition, *Ganesha* (the elephant god of Hindus) occupies a peculiar position among Jains for his popularity as the benevolent remover of all obstacles.

Briefly, Jain's art and architecture, day-to-day living, lifestyle, beliefs, and morality have been immensely influenced by Hindu traditions. Such adaptation explains how Jainism managed to survive in a predominately Hindu world. The teachings of *Gita,* the holiest book of the Hindu religion, have always been a source of inspiration to Jains. Appendix C at the end summarizes the Gita teachings.

Jainism vs. Buddhism

Buddhism emerged at the time of the twenty-fourth Jain Tirthankara Mahavira. Lord Buddha, the founder of Buddhism, was a contemporary of Tirthankara Mahavira, which means Jainism is a much older religion. In terms of philosophy, there are many similarities between Jainism and Buddhism, although there are also a number of differences. First, Jains assign more importance to austere and rigorous ascetic practices than Buddhists, who reject harsh austerities as a means for achieving enlightenment and recommend a middle way. For example, Buddhist monks symbolize their renunciation by shaving their heads; Jain monks adopt the more painful process of plucking their hair out. Second, Jains believe in the existence of the soul, whereas Buddhists do not. Third, Jains emphasize strict vegetarianism, while Buddhists do not. Finally, Jains developed their own ritualistic practices, which are much simpler and less elaborate than those followed by Buddhists.

Chapter Thirteen

Jain Religious Practices

Victory over one's self is greater than conquering thousands of enemies on the battlefield. A true conqueror is one who conquers his own self.

Jains undertake a variety of religious practices with the objective of reminding themselves of the nature of reality, their place in the universe, and their ultimate goal of shedding all Karmas and attaining absolute freedom from material bondage. It must be understood that there is a very fine line between a Jain religious practice and a ritual. In most religions, rituals are performed in the interest of achieving worldly gain, but rituals in Jainism do not have this goal. A Jain religious practice is undertaken to minimize passions, anger, pride or ego, deception or intrigue, and greed, not for material reasons or to seek absolution from sin or to escape from misery. Jain religious practices are simple and natural, free from elaborate complexities. They reflect the internal beauty and harmony of the soul and teach the idea of the supremacy of human life and the importance of a positive attitude toward life.

The message of nonviolence, truth, non-stealing, celibacy, and non-possession is one of universal compassion. A living body is not merely an integration of limbs and flesh but is also the abode of the soul, which has the potential of gaining perfect perception, perfect knowledge, perfect power, and perfect bliss. The practices reflect the freedom and spiritual joy of the living being. They emphasize that all living beings, irrespective of their size, shape, and form are equal and should be loved and respected. What is preached is the gospel of universal love.

The most common religious practices of the Jains are Jain greeting, praying at home, temple visits, religious celebrations, reading of scriptures, and pilgrimages.

Greeting

The way Jains greet one another is a part of their religious practice. The usual greeting is to fold hands in a praying position and recite the words: *"Jai Jinendra,"* meaning "Honor to the Supreme Jina." This greeting reminds the individuals to respect Jina and follow the path shown by Jina. Frequently, Jains also use the common Indian greeting *namaste,* which means "I bless the divine within you."

Praying at Home

The simplest religious practice of Jains is praying at home. Some families establish a temple at home and pray there. Others pray in any part of the home where it is quiet and they can concentrate. The prayers may be offered at any time of the day, but many Jains pray in the morning before the start of the day and again in the evening before retiring. The method of prayer varies from one individual to another. Some simply recite the Namokar Mantra nine times or 108 times, both in the morning and in the evening. Others read prayers (*pujas*) relative to one or more Tirthankaras or recite other prayers in the morning, and perform *aarti* (worship the statute of a Tirthankara with light, or *diya*) in the evening. The process of praying varies greatly between Shvetambaras and Digambaras, and Sthanakavaasis also have their own procedure.

Jainism is very flexible in the method, process, and time of offering prayers, so long as the basic objective of performing a religious practice is clearly understood.

Temple Visits

When Jains visit a temple and pray, they are not asking for material favors. Since Tirthankaras or Jinas have eliminated all desires and intentions, they cannot respond to an individual's worship. Jains pray to draw inspiration from the Tirthankaras and to become like them.

It is the Jain custom (Hindu custom as well) to remove footwear before entering the temple—or any house, for that matter. It is believed that footwear carries germs, dust, and dirt from the streets, and should not be allowed inside the temple. It is also customary for worshippers to wash their hands and legs before they enter the temple.

An image in a temple represents a symbol of perfection that points the worshipper to the spiritual goal of attaining salvation. During the course of praying in the temple, Jains psychologically perceive themselves to be face–to-face with a Tirthankara and to derive strength for seeking right perception, right knowledge, and right conduct.

Unlike Hinduism, in which a Brahamin priest is essential to mediate between the worshipper and the image, Jains perform the temple rituals themselves. (Jains do employ caretakers in the temple, but these people do not facilitate praying.) Further, Jains use very few rituals while praying, which differentiates them from Hindus, who use a number of ritual implements. Jain rituals are simple and follow no prescribed form. This allows much individual expression and interpretation.

Essentially, Jain prayers in the temple have four aspects: first, reciting the Namokar Mantra (which may be done any number of times: once, three times, nine times, twenty-one times, or even 108 times); second, singing songs praising the Tirthankaras; third, conducting Puja (a ceremonial prayer to a particular Tirthankara, following a ritualistic tradition); and fourth, performing Aarti by standing in front of the image, holding a lighted lamp, and reciting prayers specific to the occasion.

The Digambri and Shvetambri sects follow slightly different procedures in offering prayers in the temple, especially in conducting Puja as described below. Both sects, before performing Puja, require bathing and putting on clean clothes, which signifies purifying one's soul of the stains of karmic bondage. In addition, to seek separation from the profane world, each worshiper recites three times an ancient *Prakrit,* meaning "It is abandoned." Then, the worshipper bows down with hands folded, indicating submission to the Tirthankaras' teachings.

After completion of the visit to the temple, the worshipper recites three times "Aavassahi," meaning, "I go back to worldly activities."

(a) Puja Ritual: Digambari Tradition (an example of Tirthankara Mahavira's Puja)

This ceremony begins with an invocation wherein we invoke the presence of Lord Mahavira for the benefit of our spiritual development.

The invocation is followed by offerings of various substances that have symbolic meanings:

- Water: An offering of water symbolizes washing off the *wrong perception*.
- Sandalwood paste: An offering of sandalwood paste symbolizes the control and elimination of the emotion of *anger* and the stress associated with it.
- Rice: An offering of rice symbolizes the shedding of *pride*.
- Flowers: An offering of flowers symbolizes the control or elimination of *deceit* (mostly saffron-colored rice is used instead of flowers).
- Coconut: An offering of coconut symbolizes the control or elimination of *greed* and *lust*.
- Lamp: Lamp lighting signifies the elimination of *ignorance* (mostly saffron-colored cocount pieces are used).
- Burning of incense: An offering of incense symbolizes the *burning of all the Karmas* (eight primary categories) that obscure right perception, right knowledge, and right conduct.
- Fruits: An offering of fruits symbolizes the *desire to attain Nirvana*.
- Collective offering: A collective offering of all of the above symbolizes the control of anger, pride, deceit, and greed; obtaining right perception, right knowledge, and right conduct; observing penance and destroying Karmas, and thus progressing on the path to Nirvana.

The offerings are followed by singing *Jayamala*; i.e., recitation of the qualities of Tirthankara Mahavira.

After the Puja, the devotees circle three times the central chamber, where the image is placed, to symbolize right perception, right knowledge, and right conduct; and they recite devotional hymns or the Namokar Mantra.

(b) Puja Ritual: Shvetambri Tradition

- Pouring a small amount of water and bathing the image to symbolize spiritual purity.
- Applying small dots of sandalwood and saffron paste to different parts of the image to cool the passions in order to overcome Karmas (this also symbolizes the "sweet scent" of the Jina's teachings).
- Offering sweet-smelling, visually pleasing unbroken flowers to symbolize unbroken, satisfied faith in the Tirthankara's or Jina's teachings.
- Waving a stick of burning incense before the image to symbolize eradication of the "bad odor" of ignorance and worldly desire.
- Swinging a lit butter-lamp to evoke the disappearance of the darkness of ignorance in enlightenment.
- Drawing the swastika with unbroken rice.
- Placing a fruit in front of the image symbolizing the desired fruit of the ritual action, which is Nirvana.
- Placing sweets in front of the image, symbolizing giving up food (through not eating) and achieving the liberated state.

(c) <u>Prayer Halls: Sthaanakavaasi Tradition</u>

Sthaanakavaasi prayer ritual comprises sitting in a yoga position for an hour or more, reciting the Namokar Mantra, and reading scriptures. Sthaanakavaasis follow a similar process when praying at home.

(d) <u>Aarti (or Aarathi)</u>

Aarti is a ritual performed in the worship of Tirthan-karas whereby a lighted lamp is moved in a circular mo-tion clockwise around the idol. Conventionally, the lamp is moved three times to signify Right Belief, Right Knowl-edge, and Right Conduct. The sanctum is usually dark. The lighted lamp removes darkness and reveals the form of the Tirthankara when the lamp is moved all around the idol. Before electricity was invented, the only way devo-tees could see the actual idol was when the Aarti was per-formed. However, the practice of Aarti also signifies that the Tirthankara shows the path that can lead us from dark-ness to light and from ignorance to knowledge. After the Aarti, it is customary to run both the palms of one's hands over the flame and then pat the palms over one's eyes as a mark of absorbing the Tirthankara's light into the body.

Religious Celebrations

The main Jain celebrations are the birth and salva-tion of Tirthankaras, *Paryushan* or *Das Lakshana* (spiritual awareness), and *Jnaan Panchami* (day of worship of scrip-tures). The Paryushan celebration is common among Sh-vetambaras, while Digambaras around the same time of the year celebrate Das Lakshana.

Paryushan (an annual eight-day ritual followed by Shvetambaras) or *Das Lakshana* (an annual ten-day ritual followed by Digambaras) festival is celebrated with various events, elective fasting, and introspective meditation (Pratikraman) appropriate to each day's significant practice.

Among the twenty-four Tirthankaras, the birth and salvation days of the last Tirthankara, Tirthankara Mahavira, are most commonly celebrated by all Jains. The birthday of Tirthankara Mahavira falls in April, while his salvation day falls in October or November. The date may vary significantly from year to year depending on the Indian lunar calendar, which is constructed differently from the Christian calendar.

Tirthankara Mahavira attained salvation or Nirvana on the last day of the dark fortnight of the *kaartik* month in the Indian calendar. All Jains celebrate that day. Interestingly, the day has a special meaning in India as it commemorates the day Lord Rama, the Hindu deity, returned to his kingdom after spending fourteen years in the woods. All Hindus celebrate that day, which is commonly called Diwali or Deepawali, by lighting earthen lamps and candles. On the eve of Diwali, by tradition, all Hindus, including Jains, worship the goddess of wealth, Lakshmi, for good luck in the coming year (the Hindu new year begins on the day after Diwali).

(a) Paryushan or Das Lakshana:

This is probably the most important celebration among Jains. Its main purpose is spiritual awareness and comprises intense spiritual activities. Jains observe partial fasts, study scriptures, pray and worship, listen to religious discourses, and perform *pratikraman* (careful analysis of and introspection about one's past thoughts and activities). In addition, lay Jains reiterate the significance of the ultimate virtues of forgiveness, modesty, sincerity, purity of spirit, truth, and self.

Paryushan/Das Lakshana falls in August or September after the rainy season is over. There is a reason for this. Jain priests, or Sadhus, in order to avoid attachment, do not stay long in one place. But during the rainy season, which lasts four months, they do stay at one place. After the rainy season is over, and before the Sadhus depart, Paryushan or Das Lakshana is celebrated for self-reflection and in this process the presence of Sadhus is very helpful. People go over what they have learned during the time the priests stayed with them and devote eight to ten days to pray and mediate for self-awareness. On the last day, devotees visit friends and relatives for forgiveness for any wrong they might have done during the previous year.

Of the eight days of Paryushan, the first three are devoted to sermons by the priests on five activities: nonviolent living, humanitarian activities, fasting for the last three days of Paryushan, visiting temples, and repentance of one's sins, forgiving others, and seeking forgiveness from others. The remaining five days are spent reading and listening to the priests about Lord Mahavira's as well as other Tirthankaras' lives from the scripture called the *Kalpa Sutra*. In addition, on the fourth day a ceremony is performed in reverence to the *Kalpa Sutra*. On the fifth day, the auspicious dream that Lord Mahavira's mother, Trishala, had before his birth is celebrated. The last day of the Paryushan (the eighth day) is reserved for repentance of one's past sins and forgiveness to others.

As mentioned above, Das Lakshana festival lasts ten days. Each day is devoted to one religious virtue. The ten virtues are:

1. Forgiveness
   (Forgive those who did us wrong, and seek forgiveness for any personal wrongdoing)

2. Humility
   (Living humbly leads to happiness since it discourages pride and sense of superiority)

3. Straightforwardness
   (Straightforwardness in actions and thoughts enables a person to live without fear or anxiety)

4. Contentment-absence of greed
   (Deriving satisfaction from what we have rather than desiring more and more leads to contentment and hence happiness)

5. Truth
   (Truthfulness in all dealings and interactions makes a person reliable and trustworthy)

6. Restraint of all senses
   (Protecting all lives above the one-sensed creatures should be sought by controlling desires and passions)

7. Austerities
   (Avoid over-indulgence by keeping passions and desires under control)

8. Charity
   (Sharing your wealth and abilities with those who need them leads to a happy life)

9. Non-possessiveness
   (Too much attachment to material things causes undesirable traits such as anger, pride, deceit, greed, and fear)

10. Celibacy
    (Refraining from sexual and other pleasures helps keep desires in check)

The meditation during Paryushan/Das Lakshana provides laymen and laywomen an opportunity to realize themselves. During Paryushan/Das Lakshana festival a person becomes one with the light of one's soul and hence this festival is often referred to as the *Festival of the Soul*.

(b) <u>Diwali or Deepavali Celebrations:</u>

Diwali or Deepavali is India's most auspicious festival, celebrated by Hindus, Sikhs, and Jains, as well as worshippers of other religions. The most widely accepted legend for Diwali celebrations is from the Hindu epic *Ramayana*. Diwali celebrates Lord Rama's return from exile with his queen Sita and brother Lakshman to the Kingdom of Ayodhya. His subjects welcomed him with rows of lighted lamps (*deepa* or *diya* means lamp, while *vali* means row) and dispelled the long years of gloom by bathing the city in brilliant light.

The rows of *diyas* on Diwali can be interpreted in numerous positive ways. They stand for the good, which is powerful enough to shun evil. Light signifies knowledge while ignorance is symbolized by darkness. Thus, light is revered as a symbol of God.

Just as everything has evolved and changed over the years, *diyas* too have evolved through various forms. Traditionally they were baked from clay in villages across India and painted in varied hues. Decorative diyas nowadays are made of terracotta, clay, rubber, wax, and even of food items like butter and sweets. Fancier diyas are handmade and come in bright festive colors and designs. Among the most interesting types are round-shaped diyas painted in glittering gold with colored thread and mirror work on their surface. The following lines are recited upon lighting a lamp:

I salute the One who is the lamplight that brings auspiciousness, prosperity, good health, abundance of wealth, and the destruction of the intellect's enemy.

For Jains, as mentioned above, Diwali has a special meaning since the twenty-fourth Tirthankara, Mahavira, achieved Nirvana on that day. Similarly, Sikhs celebrate Diwali to welcome the return of their sixth guru (teacher). Diwali is celebrated throughout India with a great deal of pomp and show, similar to Christmas celebrations in the West. Just as in the United States, where almost everyone takes part in Christmas festivities, everyone in India, irrespective of caste or religion, is involved in some way in Diwali festivities.

Beyond the religious aspect, Diwali festival has a greater significance because the Hindu year ends that day. The new year starts the day after Diwali. Therefore, Indians, including Jains, worship the goddess of wealth, Lakshmi, on the Diwali evening. Special prayers are offered with bright oil lamps to welcome the goddess, who is believed to descend from the heavens on the day of Diwali. The Lakshmi prayer is performed in the evening, which is the ideal time for driving away evil or unpleasant forces.

Diwali falls on the last day of the dark fortnight in October/November. The celebrations, however, last for five days. Diwali time is also India's biggest shopping season for clothes, jewelry, utensils, DVD players, cell phones, cars, and other objects. People buy things for themselves as well as for gift-giving.

Among Jains, buying gold coins during Diwali and giving them to relatives or colleagues or storing them at home is an auspicious tradition. Coins are stamped with the image of Tirthankara Mahavira (or any other Tirthanakara), Lakshmi, and Ganesha. In the morning hours on the Diwali day Jains celebrate the Nirvana of Tirthankara Mahavira by visiting a nearby temple or praying at home.

Other religious rituals observed by Jains in the evening are similar to those of Hindus, where they perform goddess Lakshmi and Lord Ganesha prayers. Actual Diwali celebrations among Jains differ between Digambaras and Shvetambaras, and also from one part of the country to the other.

An inseparable part of the Diwali celebration is the creation of the Divine Design, called *rangoli. Rangoli* is the ancient Indian art, handed down through generations, of decorating walls and floors of homes with natural colors and traditional motifs made up of dots and unbroken lines. Found all over India, it is also known as *kolam* in southern India, *chowkpurana* in northern India, *madana* in

Rajasthan, *aripana* in Bihar and *alpana* in Bengal. The motifs vary according to region and occasion but lotus, swastikas, and conch shells are common everywhere. During Diwali, rangoli is meant to welcome guests and the gods—especially the goddess of wealth, Lakshmi—into homes. Lakshmi, it is believed, visits homes that are well lit and decorated. It is mostly women who do the rangoli.

On the second day after Diwali, Jains celebrate *Bhai Duj*, festival day for brothers. Legend has it that after Lord Mahavira achieved Nirvana, his brother Raja Nandivardhan missed him very much. Therefore, Lord Mahavira's sister Sudarshana invited Raja Nandivardhan to her house to comfort him. That day is celebrated as *Bhai Duj*.

Bhai Duj is similar to *Raksha Bandhan* (discussed later), with one difference. To celebrate *Raksha Bandhan,* sister visits the brother, while on Bhai Duj brother is invited by sister to her house to show her love and regard for him.

(c) <u>Other Celebrations</u>:

Jains participate in a number of other festivals and celebrations, even those that are not strictly religious. Two among them are more popular and are observed by most Jains. These are *Raksha Bandhan* and *Holi.*

Raksha Bandhan symbolizes love between brothers and sisters. The celebration involves sister tying *rakhi* (a colored thread decorated with artificial flowers and tinsels) on her brother's wrist, performing aarti and praying for his long life. The brother, on his part, takes the vow to protect the sister at all times and to come to her rescue when needed. This festival dates back to the Vedic times. It signifies the sanctity of the pious relationship that exists between brothers and sisters. Usually, Raksha Bandhan falls in the month of August.

Holi is an ancient festival of India that is colorful and joyous. It is celebrated by Hindus and non-Hindus alike, strengthening the secular fabric of the society. Holi is celebrated in two parts. On the night before the Holi festival, people accumulate firewood and place an effigy of Holika (an evil person) on a street corner. A fire is lit and the evil is reduced to ashes, symbolizing the victory of good over evil.

Legend has it that in prehistoric India there lived a powerful, evil king named Hiranyakshap who considered himself a god and wanted everybody to worship him. To his dismay, his own son, named Prahlad, began to worship Lord Vishnu instead of him. To punish his son, the king asked his sister, Holika, to enter a blazing fire with Prahlad in her lap, as she had a boon to enter fire unharmed. But the sinister scheme did not work. Prahlad's devotion to Lord Vishnu paid off. He came out of the fire unscathed while Holika was burned up. The tradition of burning firewood comes from this legend.

The second part of the Holi celebration involves play of colors in the morning. People take great pleasure in applying colored powder on each other's foreheads and faces and spraying colored water even on strangers. It is a group merrymaking event where people play with colors, offer sweets, and embrace each other to wish Happy Holi. As a part of Holi celebration, some people drink an Indian beverage called *thandai* made with milk, nuts, and sugar and laced with *bhang*, a natural intoxicating substance. Bhang helps in enhancing the spirit of the occasion.

After an eventful and fun-filled morning, people become a little sober by the afternoon. They then visit friends and relatives to greet them and exchange sweets. Often, cultural organizations plan gatherings in the afternoon and evening to generate harmony and brotherhood in the society.

Reading of Scriptures

Jain laypeople as well as monks read scriptures to gain deeper insights into the principles of Jainism. Tirthankara Mahavira's preaching was orally compiled by his immediate disciples in Jain scriptures known as *Jain Agams* or *Agama Sutras*, which consist of many texts. The Agama Sutras teach great reverence for all forms of life, strict codes of vegetarianism, asceticism, nonviolence, and opposition to war. These Agama Sutras were not documented, but have been orally passed on to future generations.

Over the course of time, many of the Agama Sutras were memorized and some were modified. About one thousand years after they were memorized, the Agama Sutras were recorded on leafy paper. Most Jains accept these sutras as an authentic version of Tirthankara Mahavira's teachings. The twelve major Agama Sutras are:

1) *Acara*, a treatise on the life of Tirthankara Mahavira and the rules of behavior for a monk.
2) *Satrakrta*, which purports to clarify and counter prevailing heresies.
3) *Sthana* (cases), an encyclopedia treatise on Jain doctrines presented in a numerical fashion, beginning with one and concluding with ten, so as to render it more accessible to readers.

4) The *Samavaya*, which continues the wide-ranging discourses of the third Agama, while intoning the fullest summary of all the Agamas, combined.

5) The *Vyakhyaprajnapti*, also known as *Bhagavati*, consists of forty-one chapters on an enormous canvas—philosophy, ethics, mathematics, theory of knowledge, and cosmology. Much of it was written in the form of questions and answers between Tirthankara Mahavira and his disciple, Gautama Swami.

6) *Jnatadharmakatha*, pertaining to questions on morality, and written essentially for laypersons.

7) The *Upasakada* treatises lay-votaries and their observances.

8) *Antakrddasa* is devoted to the explication of liberated souls. It traces the *tapas,* or austerities, undertaken by various ascetics.

9) *Anuttaraupapatikadasa* treats the specific instances of reincarnations.

10) The *Prasnavyakarana* is focused on the perilous itineraries of karma.

11) The *Vipakasruta* analyses causality with respect to the outcome of our actions, both good and bad.

12) The *Drstivada* manuscript has been lost.

Pilgrimages

Jains undertake pilgrimages to different temples. Jain temples are famous for their architecture, art, and sculptures. The carvings, which can be found both inside and outside many temples, are masterpieces of sculpture. Most temples were built between the eleventh and thirteenth centuries AD.

There are more than three hundred major Jain temples and holy sites. The map in illustration 11 lists the twenty-eight most popular places for pilgrimage. Among these, the following are probably the most religiously noteworthy and the ones that most Jains hope to visit during their lifetime.

a) Between #11 and #12 on the map: Girnar Mountain (Gujarat)—Tirthankara Neminatha attained Nirvana from here[4]

b) #26 Temple Melsitamur at Tirumalai (Tamilnadu)

c) #7 Chittorgarh Fort (Rajasthan)

d) #16 Kundalpur (Madhya Pradesh)

e) #4 Padamura at Sadri (Rajasthan)

f) #3 Mahavirji (Rajasthan)

g) #12 Shatrunjaya Hill (Gujarat): also known as Palitana

h) #5 Ranakpur (Rajasthan)

i) Near #6 Sirohi in the map: Delwada Temple—Mount Abu (Rajasthan)

j) Near #17 Rajgir in the map: Sammed Shikharji (Bihar)—Twenty Tirthankaras attained salvation from here

k) #18 Mahavira Mandir: Pavapuri (Bihar)—Tirthankara Mahavira attained Nirvana from here

l) #24 Shravanabelagola (Karnatak)

---

4   *The numbers here, as well as those that follow, refer to the numbers in the map in Illustration 11. The Indian state is given within parentheses.*

Subhash C. Jain

Illustration 11
Select Jain Places of Pilgrimage

1- LADNUN	15 – PAVAGIRI (UN)
2 - MATHURA	16 - KUNDALPUR
3 - MAHAVIRJI	17 - RAJGIR
4 - SADRI	18 - PAVAPURI
5 - RANAKPUR	19 - CHAMPAPUR
6 - SIROHI	20 - AIHOLE
7 - CHITTORGARH	21 - BADAMI
8 - SONAGIRI	22 - KARKALA
9 - IDAR	23 - MOODABIDRI
10 - SHANKESHVARA	24 - SHRAVANABELAGOLA
11 - BHADRESHWAR	25 - HALEBID
12 - PALITANA	26 - TIRUMALAI
13 - MANGI-TUNGI	27 - TIRUNARUNGKONDAI
14 - CHULAGIRI	28 - SITTANNAVASAL

Chapter Fourteen

Jain Meditation[5]

When a person commits a sinful deed, whether intentionally or unintentionally, he should immediately withdraw from that with the resolve that such an act would not be committed again.

The purpose of Jain meditation is to stop the inflow of karmic particles and to shed existing karmic matter so that the true nature of the immortal soul manifests itself. Meditation should be practiced daily for about 20 minutes to 48 minutes.

The meditation procedure requires that you sit in a relaxed posture. Then, practice breathing by inhaling, retaining, and exhaling in the ratio of 1:2:1, i.e., inhale with a count of eight, then retain the breath with a count of 16, and exhale with a count of eight. This exercise should be repeated 12 times. At this time you will begin to relax, and you should contemplate your daily life following the structure given below:

A. Initial checklist
- I adore the Three Jewels
  - Right Faith or Perception or Belief
  - Right Knowledge
  - Right Conduct

---

5   *This method of meditation has been suggested by Gurudev Chitrabhanuji.*

- I shall have with humility
  - Amity for all
  - Compassion for those below
  - Appreciation for those above
  - Equanimity for those who cannot hear the teaching
- I radiate light to everyone and everything
  - Through infinite Knowledge, infinite Perception, infinite Bliss and infinite Energy

B. Main checklist
  - Positive nonviolence (Ahimsa): Meditate on anger, pride, and greed
    - Was I nonviolent towards others and toward myself in thought? In word? In action?
    - Did I encourage or appreciate violence in others?
    - Did I impose my thoughts on another?
    - Did I use my position to manipulate someone (a position of strength or a position of weakness)?
    - Did I speak harshly?
    - Was I selfish, competitive, insecure, and fearful?
    - Did I put any harmful substance into my body (e.g., junk food, excess sugar)?
    - Did I expose my mind to violence in the form of movies, TV, books, wrong company?
  - Truthfulness (Satya): Meditate on deceit
    - Was I truthful toward others and toward myself in thought? In word? In action?

- Did I encourage or appreciate non-truthful-ness in another?
- Did I exaggerate or distort the facts for personal gain?
- Did I use flattery or act pretentiously to get what I desire?
- Whatever I speak will be the truth, but I need not reveal all the truth.
- Trust must not create violence.

• Non-Stealing (Asteya): Meditate on insecurity
  - Did I speak truth in whatever I said?

• Celibacy (Brahmacharya): Meditate on insincerity
  - Did I practice celibacy? In thought? In word? In action?
  - Was I lustful? (dwell on sensuality)
  - Did I encourage or appreciate lustfulness in others?
  - Did I waste sexual energy on sexual fantasies?
  - Did I use my sexual energies to manipulate others? (e.g., flirting)

• Non-possessiveness (Aparigraha): Meditate on greed and jealousy
  - Was I non-acquisitive or non-possessive? In thought? In word? In action?
  - Did I encourage or appreciate acquisition and possessiveness in others?
  - Do I have possessive attachments to people or things?
  - Do I have things around that I am not using? Am I collecting or hoarding?
  - Did I buy something today that I do not need?

Many people want to practice mediation but fall prey to the demands of life. It is important to realize that when you decide to meditate, you are making a commitment to life, and particularly to its quality. You also make a commitment to bliss, because bliss and discipline are interlinked. Even though most people are aware of that, they find a hectic life tripping up their good intentions. The best way to practice mediation is to integrate it into your daily routine. That was the way meditation was practiced in ancient times. The warrior used it to hone his strength and skill, the king to rule with wisdom, the courtesan to enamor her lovers, the wife to keep her husband entranced. The monks used it to achieve self-realization.

Meditation is a practical tool that enhances skill in whatever you wish to do. If we find we cannot practice regularly, it may be because we treat meditation as an exercise routine for which we must make time. Like the ancients, we need to make it part of our *life*.

While there is a formal procedure for meditation, you can adopt a flexible routine to meditate. You can practice meditation if you are being driven around or using public transport. Sitting on a chair at work or at home, you can meditate by chanting *Namokar Mantra* and trying to lock your mind to it by repeating it constantly. You will see the mind refuses to be pinned down. This exposes a fallacy of free will, since the mind runs wild on its own. The trick is not to shut the mind down, but to watch its helter-skelter movements from the perch of Namokar Mantra. This focus is a powerful *sadhana* (individual practice).

Chapter Fifteen

A Demographic Profile of Jains

Do your duty and do it as humanly as you can—this, in brief, is the primary principle of Jainism.

According to the 2001 census of India, there are 12.5 million Jains in the world. Unofficial estimates of the Jain community specify a slightly larger number of 15 million. In the context of India's one billion people, Jains constitute a very small percentage (about 1.5 percent). Yet they play a significant role in all spheres of life in India such as commerce, the professions (law, medicine), education, politics, the arts, and culture.

About 83 percent of Jains live in five Indian states (Maharashtra, Gujarat, Rajasthan, Madhya Pradesh, and Karnataka). Other important centers of Jain population are Uttar Pradesh, Delhi, Tamil Nadu, West Bengal, and Haryana.

There are about 350,000 Jains who live outside India. Of them, about 200,000 make their homes in the United States, where the majority are concentrated in nine states, which, in order of importance are—New York, California, New Jersey, Michigan, Illinois, Texas, Maryland, Ohio, and Massachusetts.

About one-third of all Jains have the last name Shah, while about 15 percent use Jain as their last name. Other common last names among Jains are Mehta, Doshi, Sheth, Vora, Kothari, and Gandhi.

Jains have the highest literacy rate among all Indians, 94.1 percent. Despite the high literacy among Jain females, fewer than 10 percent of them work outside the home. Over three-quarters of all Jains live in urban areas.

Chapter Sixteen

The Uniqueness of the Jain Religion

Non-violence is the best guarantee of humanity's survival and progress. A truly non-violent man is ever awake and is incapable of harboring any ill will.

This chapter is written especially for the new generation of Jains, born and raised in North America and other foreign countries. Preserving and enhancing a minority culture in a different or foreign environment requires diligence and perseverance. Most of the 350,000 Jains living outside India have faced some challenge at one time or another. The United States was founded on the idea of religious freedom for all. Here there is freedom to practice what we believe in. But many attitudes and well-accepted traditions in Western societies are different from those found in Jain culture.

The common practice of dating jeopardizes the aspect of partial celibacy. Dating, generally, promotes premarital sex, which is against the Jain culture. When youngsters choose their marriage partners without consulting their parents, there is an increased distance between the generations. If the marriage is successful, generational estrangement is avoided, but if there are difficulties, divorce is likely unless there is parental support. Divorce is so easy in this society that people forget that compromise, tolerance, and understanding are needed to preserve a marriage.

Elderly people living by themselves or in institutions, waiting to see their children and grandchildren, is undesirable. Grandparents taking care of grandchildren on a daily basis is a routine sight in the Jain community. The role of the elderly in the extended family is that of caregiver and adviser. The presence of this older generation is important in the upbringing of children and in providing stability for the whole family.

The constant quest for material goods and excessive consumption in this society conflict with the Jain principle of nonpossessiveness. A materialistic view affects the cohesiveness of the family. If even within a family, items and "territory" are kept separate, young children do not learn the value of sharing, and they are further influenced by a society in which sharing is not emphasized. In the Jain tradition, sharing is instilled as an important character trait at an early age.

The greatest problem in the present culture is the emphasis placed on the individual. In the United States, culture revolves around the self. Everyone expects personal freedom. This principle, however, has been abused to the extent that decisions are made without respect to the well-being of the family. In contrast, Jain tradition and culture place emphasis on the family.

Why Should I Admire My Religion?

Jains born and raised outside India should take pride in their religion because it is thoroughly modern in outlook, despite the fact that it is steeped in a rich and ancient tradition. Here are a few points that should enhance your admiration of your religion.

a. Relations with the World

Jains look at the world through the eyes of humane stewards. Consistent with the fundamental principle of Ahimsa, Jains attempt to practice nonviolence in their encounters with other people, animals, and the environment. No other ancient tradition has more consistently resisted the unfortunate human tendency toward aggression and militarism. In this era of recurring wars, excessive materialism, ecological destruction, and gross violation of human and animal rights, one would be hard-pressed to find a value more greatly needed in the modern world than nonviolence. Jainism offers this value.

b. Importance of Education

Jains place an exceptionally high value on learning, knowledge, and rationality. But unlike many other traditions that view science and religion as being in essential conflict, the Jain worldview incorporates modern scientific thinking and realizes the potential benefits of technology wisely used.

c. Elevation of Democratic Principles

Thousands of years before the French Revolution, Jains espoused and practiced the doctrine that all human beings should be treated as equals. Rejecting the historically concurrent and widespread infliction of slavery, the caste system, the subordination of women, and the sacrifice of humans and animals, Jains long ago set an egalitarian example that still serves as a beacon of enlightenment for advocates of a democratic philosophy.

Briefly, there is a long history of public discussion and dissent among Jains. The point may be made with reference to all-conquering Alexander's experience with Jain monks as he roamed around northwest India around 325 BC. He came across a group of Jain monks, who neglected to pay any attention to him. Alexander was clearly disappointed and questioned them about their lack of interest in him. The head of the monk group gave the following reply:

King Alexander, every man can possess only so much of the earth's surface as this we are standing on. You are but human like the rest of us, save that you are always busy and up to no good, traveling so many miles from your home, a nuisance to yourself and to others!...You will soon be dead, and then you will own just as much of the earth as will suffice to bury you.

Subsequently, it is believed that King Alexander returned to Greece

d. <u>Tolerance for Dissenting Opinion</u>

Most religious and philosophical traditions have shown a regrettable propensity for dogmatism and prejudice toward those who hold dissenting opinions and values. Although deeply rooted in solid conviction, Jains have resolutely cultivated a system that acknowledges the relativity of knowledge and resists the temptation to arrogantly view one's group as the only people chosen to carry "the truth" to the world. The Jain perspective readily admits that non-Jains have made important contributions to the development of ethics, religion, philosophy, society, and other areas of activity.

e. Respect for the Arts

In societies such as the United States, the importance of artistic inspiration and expression are, at best, compartmentalized into a role subordinate to that of science, technology, and commerce. In the language of cognitive psychology, Westerners place greater value on "left-brain" modes of thinking—those that emphasize linear and analytic modes of perception—than on "right-brain" modes of thinking—those that are characterized by holistic and intuitive modes of perception. Jains understand that these two ways of processing information need to be balanced for the optimal evolution of human potential. In the service of that ideal, art, sculpture, music, dance, and even architecture have played a central and honored role in the manifestation of Jain tradition. Art is seen neither as the exclusive province of the elite nor as a segregated activity with no practical relevance to daily living. Through artistic creativity, the sublime can be injected into daily activities, and the past can be kept alive in the present.

f. Honoring Spiritual Values

Jainism has much to teach us about the spiritual quest because for thousands of years it has brought forth wise masters (the Tirthankaras) who have devoted their lives to this most important of inquiries: What is our ultimate identity and most fundamental relationship to the universe of which we are an expression?

Jains hold ancient wisdom in high regard but have a healthy respect for scientific discovery and rational debate; they are vigorous and consistent proponents of their values, yet they exercise humility and tolerance for persons of different persuasions; they are not preoccupied with materialism, but are successful at securing the practical, financial means for a good quality of living and are most generous in sharing their resources with others. Although Jains are serious critics of injustice and exploitation, on a personal level they maintain the congenial attitude that life is a divine gift to be enjoyed by all.

Jains believe that every individual soul has the potential of being a god, which state comes when the soul has attained Nirvana. Everybody can attain godhood by making supreme efforts in the right direction. The emphasis is on the individual's action to attain Nirvana (*Moksha*, or salvation). Salvation is to be attained by one's own efforts. All souls are alike. None is superior or inferior. A Jain's main aim in this life is to strive for the liberation of the soul from the cycle of death and rebirth and to achieve Nirvana, a state of eternal bliss and knowledge.

Ahimsa (nonviolence and non-injury toward all living beings) is the cornerstone of Jainism and strict vegetarianism is an integral part of this principle. Jains believe in reincarnation based on cause and effect (the law of Karma).

Jainism's guiding lights are the "three jewels": right faith (or right perception), right knowledge, and right conduct. Living by these three principles, Jains try not to harm any living creature, to be absolutely truthful, not to steal, to be chaste in thought and deed, and to practice nonattachment to the world by strictly limiting possessions. The following are the principal tenets of Jainism.

- JAINS' IDENTITY
  - Jains are the followers of Jinas (victors)
  - Jinas have attained victory over their inner enemies
- INNER ENEMIES
  - Anger, pride, ego, deceit, greed
- BEGINNING
  - Jains believe that Jainism has always existed. There is at least 8,000 years of documented history
- MAIN PRINCIPLES and BELIEFS
  - Ahimsa (nonviolence)
  - Anekantvad (nonabsolutism)
  - Interdependence (of all life universally)
  - Equanimity (togetherness)
  - Compassion, Empathy, and Charity
- CONCEPT of GOD
  - Jains do not believe in God as a creator, destroyer, or preserver
  - Every soul in its purest form is a god
  - Every life form is equal and is able to become god
  - The way to become a god is to rid oneself of all Karmas, good and bad
- KARMA THEORY
  - The soul is like a magnet
  - Karmas are like iron particles
  - All actions, good or bad, attract these particles to the soul
  - The ultimate goal is to get rid of all these particles (demagnetization)
  - This is accomplished through rational perception, rational knowledge, and rational conduct

- PROPHETS
  - The prophets in Jainism are called Tirthankaras
  - There are twenty-four Tirthankaras
  - Jains follow the teachings of the last Tirthankara, Mahavira Swami or Bhagwan Mahavira (599 BC–527 BC), who is credited with reinventing Jainism
- TEXTS and SCRIPTURES
  - The main Jain scriptures are called "Agamas"—forty-five volumes (according to some, thirty-six) that constitute the teachings of Lord Mahavira; among them, the twelve are major Agamas
  - There are many other works by noted scholars throughout history that treat the details of every aspect of life

Chapter Seventeen

Living Happily

By conquering greed, contentment is achieved.

Happiness is something all humans desire, but it is a state of mind that does not come easily. Even the richest and the mightiest may not feel happy. Why does this situation occur? Religious leaders and psychologists point out routes to happiness, yet there appear to be few common denominators. People in developing countries cite poverty as the root cause of their unhappiness. Using the absence of poverty as a criterion, the United States, with its abundance of material wealth, should be replete with happiness. But this is not so; apparently there is no causal relationship between material well-being and happiness. Based on the exchange of ideas, and brainstorming sessions with a number of scholars and religious leaders, presumably the following paths lead to happiness.

Praying

For a happy life, Jains should pray daily, both in the morning upon rising and just before retiring for the night. Even praying for a few seconds seems to be beneficial if done on a regular basis. Praying helps motivate an individual to do the right things even when he is tempted to do otherwise. The result is a feeling of goodness and self-worth. Feeling good about oneself generates happiness.

A belief in Tirthankaras, monks, and sages influences how one faces difficulty. If misunderstood or falsely accused, a person can find comfort by reciting Namokar Mantra. Ultimately, the truth prevails, goodness is rewarded, and evil is punished. The net result is, you feel happy.

Human life runs in cycles. There are good times and bad times. In the good times, praying prevents one from being carried into undesirable activities. In the bad times, praying encourages a person to take heart, to persevere until the cycle brings the good times back again. In the midst of trouble, people need hope if they are to maintain their happiness or, if it has been lost, to find it again. Praying is an act of faith, and it engenders hope.

Praying is a tool for doing right, seeing right, and hearing right. But what exactly is praying? For Jains, praying is following the path traveled by Tirthankaras, that is, developing the virtues of the Tirthankaras. How should one pray? It helps to recite some worlds from one's religious text to concentrate in prayer. Essentially, for Jains the simplest way is to recite Namokar Mantra.

A prayer may last a few seconds or continue for minutes or even hours, but what seems to matter most is praying with full concentration. For example, you may recite Namokar Mantra three times, nine times, 108 times or many multiples of 108. In today's vocabulary, it is the quality rather than the quantity that counts.

Through prayers we seek happiness, and we should bear in mind as we pray that happiness does not depend on money alone but on a wholesome life. We should pray for a well-balanced life, one filled with purpose, peace, and joy. We should pray to be a blessing to others and to accomplish in this world whatever we intended to achieve.

Praying creates a state of mind that is conducive to happy living. Rich people are often not happy, but happy people are truly rich.

Exercising

"Health is wealth," as the saying goes. No matter how rich, powerful, or creative you are, if you don't have good health, it is hard to be happy. Good health is a function of many variables, including genetics, but regular exercise is one of the most important.

Exercise helps maintain mental as well as physical health. It refreshes memory, broadens horizons, and enhances creativity. Someone who exercises feels active and alert—attitudes that make for a more attractive personality and a more attractive body. As others of both sexes react positively to good looks and personality, the result is increased happiness. Consider military personnel anywhere in the world. Their day starts with exercise because exercise is basic to being physically and mentally fit. They are capable of handling the responsibility of defending their nation because they maintain a positive attitude based on the knowledge of their fitness.

Human bodies are like machines in that they must be serviced routinely if they are to run in mint condition. Regular exercise is the best way to service the body. Not only does exercising help prevent illness, it also nourishes the mind, making a person feel young and enthusiastic. Those who work out regularly generally perform better at their jobs than those who do not exercise. For this reason the Japanese often mandate exercise as a part of the workday's activities.

To derive full benefit from exercising, you must do it regularly. Intermittent exercise is not likely to be helpful. Indeed, engaging only occasionally in an intensive program may actually be counterproductive, because of the increased likelihood of injury. What is needed is a balanced program of exercise at least three times a week.

Exercising supports the Jain principle of equanimity. It encourages accommodation and attitude of the phrase "live and let live."

Vegetarian Diet

"Sound body, sound mind" is an old saying. Vegetarianism is probably the easiest way to maintain a sound body. Historically, dietary habits have been based on available food. For example, people living on the coast consumed seafood. By the same token, inhabitants of river basins commonly ate fish. Those residing on fertile fields depended on agricultural products such as grains, vegetables, and fruits. People on cattle ranches ate a lot of red meat. In the modern world, what a person eats has nothing to do with location, because refrigerated transportation makes most foods available. Virtually anywhere in the United States it is possible to buy apples grown in New Zealand, oranges from Spain, and tomatoes from Mexico.

Religion is one variable that may dictate what foods can be consumed. Although most religions are silent on this point, no religion demands the killing and eating of animals. Jainism specifically prohibits killing animals. Thus as a Jain, on faith itself you should be a vegetarian.

Being a vegetarian has many advantages. Foremost among them is health. A vegetarian diet consisting of fruits, vegetables, and grains is the healthiest diet known. Some dieticians argue that meat is necessary for protein, but close examination shows that different kinds of beans have as much protein as any type of meat. Vegetarian meals are simple to prepare and easy to digest. With the right types of seasoning, a vegetarian preparation can be as tasty as any meat dish. A vegetarian diet is light, so one never feels stuffed; consequently, vegetarians always feel active and alert. The side effects of vegetarianism are all positive and are conducive to happiness.

Another argument in favor of vegetarianism is that is avoids the killing of innocent animals. Any living being feels pain when attacked, yet we attack and kill animals for our eating pleasure. Some animals kill each other in order to eat, and humans behave like animals when they do the same. It is horrible to realize humans kill animals, remove their skin, wash the blood off, cut the body into pieces, cook the pieces, and eat them. Such behavior is undignified. Knowing one's life is based on killing the innocent must detract from happiness.

Arguments in favor of vegetarianism raise the question of why, if it is so good, the majority of people in the world eat meat. The reason is that over time people have become addicted to meat and they find it difficult to change. Besides, there are business interests that wholeheartedly promote meat products.

Vegetarians are more likely to be at peace with themselves than carnivores. A vegetarian will have the internal strength and willpower to face calamities that non-vegetarians lack. A vegetarian is more likely to have pure thoughts that lead to creativity. No matter how one looks at it, vegetarianism makes life feel wholesome and happy. Not many people who have been carnivores all their life are going to become vegetarians simply because it is one path that leads to happiness, but the fact remains that meat eating is totally undesirable.

Abstaining from Drinking and Smoking

Drinking and smoking are two vices that have existed from the beginning of civilization; they are common to all societies, cultures, and economic groups. Practically all nations have some laws to restrict drinking and smoking, especially among the young. It is widely accepted that these substances are harmful to health and yet their consumption is not banned anywhere except, in the case of drinking, in Islamic cultures. Even there, however, drinking does occur under some circumstances. The reason drinking and smoking continue to be allowed is that they have such a strong social and entertainment component.

Of the two habits, smoking is considered to be more detrimental to physical health than drinking. Smoking has been found to be the leading cause of cancer, heart trouble, and other fatal diseases. Even indirect smoke can be injurious to a person's health.

With regard to the psychological effects that determine a person's happiness, drinking has much greater potential for harm. Moderate drinking on social occasions causes no difficulties, and in some cultures it is common to have wine with dinner. But excessive drinking causes people to drive at high speeds, lose track of time and space, squander money on alcohol that should be spent on other things, and enter into abusive arguments that result in accidents, fights, and domestic problems. Diseases, including cirrhosis of the liver and heart damage, result from long-term abuse of alcohol.

People who seek happiness through Jainism should give up smoking and drinking. It is because production of any type of drink involves killing of bacteria. Thus, even social drinking for Jains is not desirable. This is a prescription that will sharpen the mind, reduce irritating behavior, and maintain good health, all of which will lead to happiness.

Pursuing Hobbies and Special Interests

People who have a hobby or special interest to pursue are more likely to experience joy and fulfillment than those without such diversions. It is a good idea to have both an indoor and an outdoor hobby. In places where winters are harsh and long, a person needs a hobby that can be pursued indoors and an outside interest, which coincidentally promotes good health by exposing one to fresh air and sunlight.

Some hobbies involve more than one person, while others can be enjoyed alone. If a person is unable to find others to engage in a group activity, an alternative one should be selected that can be pursued individually.

Further, a hobby should be entered into for entertainment and relaxation and should not become a burden. Don't follow a hobby to please someone else; don't consider it a duty. Pursue a hobby when you have the time and the mood. It is something to do for pleasure. Adding pleasure to life adds happiness. Hobbies create compassion and empathy for others.

Lifelong Education

Traditionally, education takes place in the early years before one enters the job market, but in the last thirty years, people have also come to realize that education never ends; it is a continuing process. The world around us is changing so fast that most jobs today require us to pursue education on an ongoing basis. But the advantages of continuing education are not only job-related. They extend to personal life as well and contribute greatly to happiness.

Education broadens mental horizons. It makes a person more aware of the surrounding world. It inspires self-confidence by making one feel intellectually capable and in tune with the environment. Continuing education puts you in a social environment with others who are also eager to learn. Unlike most regular schooling (including college education), there is no pressure and people are pursuing the subjects they enjoy. Such an atmosphere is conducive to happiness.

Lifelong education can continue even after formal retirement. Acquiring new knowledge is satisfying at any stage of life. You gain self-respect when you realize that you are still an active person learning new things. The age-related problems of loneliness and lack of purpose are successfully combated by continuing education. Any education is good since it leads to new insights about life and helps us realize that truth is relative.

Marital Relationships

Marriage is probably the most sacred relationship that can exist between two individuals. Traditionally, it has been a lifelong commitment with few exceptions. Today the divorce rate in many societies exceeds 50 percent. Nevertheless, studies repeatedly confirm the higher probability of happiness within marriage, and most unmarried people seek the married state.

When a husband and wife have similar goals, life is more likely to be happy. Of course, even when two people have much in common, they may approach some areas of life differently. Therefore, for happier living, both partners should be willing to adapt to each other's likes and dislikes, interests and hobbies, and approaches to family problems. In other words, for the sake of happiness husbands and wives should be able to make adjustments and accept compromises. They also should be able to trust each other with their deepest thoughts and concerns. Without mutual trust and open communication, marriage can be a force for unhappiness.

In the past, the division of labor within a marriage was clear. The wife stayed home, reared the children, and managed the household. The husband went into the world and supported the family financially. With boundaries clearly defined, each had a territory in which to excel without competing with the other. Today, the roles have changed and conflicts between husbands and wives are far more likely to occur. When both work outside the home, they may compete and disagree about handling responsibilities.

There are various ways couples can make adjustments to these modern problems. Either the husband or the wife could work only part-time while the other would provide the principal source of income. Or one might volunteer to stay home while the other earns the living.

Happiness flourishes when a satisfactory partnership exists, but this satisfaction requires tolerance and commitment in thought, word, and deed.

Service to the Community

Human beings are social animals, with a need for belonging and for feeling a part of a community. This feeling of kinship, however, is not spontaneous; it must be formed and managed. The existence of any community is possible only when its constituents (the people who belong or aspire to belong) are willing to contribute to its existence. Being a contributing member of a community satisfies a deep-seated human need and thus enhances the chances of happiness.

Service to a community generally takes three forms: money, time, and effort. Most people lack the discretionary income to make substantial contributions of money or the leisure to make lengthy contributions of time. However, almost anyone can contribute some effort, to help the community.

In the modern world, everyone seems to be extremely busy. Yet somehow there must be found the flexibility to devote time to the community. We come into this world emptyhanded and leave emptyhanded. What one achieves in this life is to a large extent a function of the social, political, economic, and community environment. The community is directly or indirectly responsible for our achievements. We are, therefore, duty bound to repay it for what it has given us. Unlike the taxes that we must pay, contributions to the community are voluntary, and there is no penalty for failing to contribute, but when we do contribute, that action can give us immense pleasure. We feel ourselves to be responsible citizens, giving as well as receiving, and this awareness brings self-respect and fulfillment, leading to real happiness. Service to the community is useful for minimizing greed and promotes social equity and justice.

Realistic Ambition

Often one hears that you have to be ambitious; that you must "get ahead." In order to achieve anything, you have to have a dream; you have to aim high. While there is some truth in these sayings, ambitions, dreams, and aims must be within a person's means and abilities. Unrealistic goals end in frustration and unhappiness.

Few people can ever become president of the United States. Few people make it to the Olympics and even fewer win gold medals. Not everyone has what it takes to be a movie star, a professional athlete, or a Nobel Prize winner. Not every artist will become famous; not every writer will produce a bestseller. Not every manager will become a CEO. There are inherent strengths that are prerequisites to achieving those heights. If you lack those traits, you will need to aim for something within your reach.

A person's success, irrespective of the field or profession, is said to depend on five factors: talent, charisma, opportunity, effort, and luck. Talent and charisma are inborn. With opportunity and an effort to capitalize on them, talent and charisma will flourish. And if luck is in your favor, you can have much. Even with luck, opportunity, and effort, without talent or charisma one can go only so far.

People should study their strengths and weaknesses when they are setting their goals and realistically consider what is possible for them to achieve. If one is fortunate enough to achieve more than one expected, so much the better. When we hear success stories, we tend to ignore the talent that existed and the effort that was made and instead attribute the accomplishment to luck alone. People who set goals are far more likely to achieve something in life than those who just wait for the wave of luck.

You should aspire to achieve the very best that is feasible, given the talents and charisma you possess and assuming you will have average opportunity and luck. The vow of "seek and speak truth" in the Jain code of conduct comes in handy here. One should be honest with oneself in evaluating strengths and weaknesses in the process of setting goals.

Sharing Wealth

We all need money to buy the basic necessities as well as to acquire goods and services for safety and ego satisfaction. But what do you do with money when you have everything you ever wanted? Empirical studies have shown that increases in income and happiness parallel each other up to a point but that a level of saturation is reached where increased wealth no longer guarantees increased happiness. In other words, there is a limit to the congruence of wealth and happiness.

What do many people who have reached that limit do to increase their happiness? This is a common question that a large proportion of Americans are trying to answer today. In the years since World War II there has been such an increase in wealth that many Americans no longer want more material goods; they now look for assets that will create lasting happiness. In those parts of the world in which all but a small percentage of people lack adequate nutrition and other necessities, material welfare is the key to happiness, but this situation does not exist in a country where even the poor are rich by standards of an earlier time or by those of today's Third World. This is the case in America today.

Achieving happiness in the midst of plenty is feasible, but not simple. It requires a new perspective. Reaching this perspective has two prerequisites. First, renounce comparing wealth with material goods. Constant comparison with those who are smarter, more beautiful, or more successful tends to breed envy, frustration, and unhappiness. Reflect instead on all the things you have. It is possible to increase feelings of satisfaction by comparing yourself with those less fortunate.

Second, limit your desires to those things that directly contribute to your physical, mental, and emotional health. Dennis Tito paid $20 million to go for a space trip. Extravagance like that needs to be controlled.

Wealth should be used in the interests of spirituality and enlightenment, which requires using wealth for the welfare of others. You should try to consider your excess wealth as the wealth that belongs to society. A person with great riches is simply someone who is entrusted with the task of using the excess for the benefit of the society. It may be used to benefit the world's children who suffer from malnutrition; it may be used locally to rejuvenate your own city or town. In other words, wealth can be used in many ways to generate happiness.

Charitable giving is common among Jains. But enlarging the scope of your giving can do more. In a globalized world, it is possible to go beyond adding to the coffers of an already rich university. Wealth can reduce poverty and sickness among the less fortunate. The more directly your donations target the truly poor, the more happiness you will derive. Non-possessiveness, one of the principles of Jainism, is directly relevant here.

Disciplined Life

Above all, happiness belongs to those whose lives are disciplined in all respects. Discipline applies to daily routines such as when you sleep, what you eat, and when you pray and exercise, to work habits, and to leisure-time activities. Discipline leads to accomplishments that bring fulfillment and happiness, which result in a life full of excitement and challenge. A disciplined person wants to do whatever is possible. Naturally, such a person will be happy and contented.

To lead a disciplined life you must be self-assured and have the courage to say *no* to certain things even if it means some people will not like you. It should not matter if they disapprove. You should lead your life so that you are happy. If friends are upset that you can't go for a drink after work because it conflicts with something that you want to do, let it be. You must have the courage of your convictions.

It is not necessary to be antisocial or impolite in order to maintain a disciplined life. As a matter of fact, it is important to preserve a flexible attitude. There may be occasions when you will have to give up a routine in order to deal with an emergency. What is necessary is to not surrender to momentary pleasures at the cost of your life's agenda. A disciplined life is not an inflexible life, but rather one in which priorities are recognized and in which lesser pleasures are sacrificed for more durable ones.

Postscript

Any activity of thought, speech, or action that helps us get rid of our inner enemies (anger, pride, ego, greed and deceit) is a Jain activity.

Jainism is about discipline and observance. It is an eminently practical philosophy, as Gandhi brilliantly proved. Mahatma Gandhi said that three persons had influenced him deeply: Tolstoy, Ruskin, and Raychandbhai. To highlight the spirit and essence of Jainism, below are the words exchanged between Mahatma Gandhi and Raychandbhai, who was one of the greatest Jain personalities of the nineteenth century.

Gandhi: If a snake is about to bite me, should I allow myself to be bitten or should I kill it, supposing that is the only way in which I can save myself?

Raychandbhai: One hesitates to advise you that you should let the snake bite you. Nevertheless, how can it be right for you, if you have realized that the body is perishable, to kill, for protecting a body which has no real value to you, a creature which clings to its own life with great attachment? For anyone who desires his spiritual welfare, the best course is to let his body perish in such circumstances. But how should a person who does not desire spiritual welfare behave? My only reply to such a question is, how can I advise such a person that he should pass through hell and similar worlds, that is, that he should kill the snake? If the person lacks the development of a noble character, one may advise him to kill the snake, but we should wish that neither you nor I will even dream of being such a person.

I end this book with the new year greetings of Gurudev Chitrabhanuji, one of the most distinguished Jain scholars of our time.

The flow of time is unceasing. We can use our precious and passing moments to nourish and enrich our hearts by loving ourselves and all living beings.

May amity permeate our entire being, soothing us like a healing balm so that, in turn, we soothe others.

Let us delve deeper into ourselves and feel the celestial and gentle core of love. The experience will bring to our lives kindness and beauty and will infuse in our hearts the warmth that can melt away the sress of Hatred, Antagonism and Resentment.

Let love renew our life and bring to it freshness and joy. Let shine through: a friendly smile, a sincere word, a loving action.

Not the New Day alone, but may every throb of our life be a moment of loving happiness.

APPENDICES

Appendix A

Indic Civilization: A Historical Perspective

The *Oxford English Dictionary* defines civilization as "a developed or advanced state of human society." Before examining the history of Indic civilization, it is desirable to consider the beginning of human civilization. According to Western scholars, Jericho, located west of the Euphrates River, was the cradle of civilization, where agriculture had developed to provide food for the region's inhabitants before 6000 BC. But this had been considered an abstract example. The recognizable beginning of civilization was in Mesopotamia. Starting with Mesopotamia, here is the rough chronology of the world's civilizations:

(a) Mesopotamian, 3500 BC
(b) Indic, 2500 BC
(c) Minoan, 2000 BC
(d) Chinese, 1800 BC
(e) Mesoamerican, 1500 BC

Beyond 1500 BC, no civilization had been identified which developed independently without the stimulus, shock, or inheritance provided by the preceding civilizations.

The Ancient World

The Mesopotamian civilization flourished in the southern part of the area, a seven-hundred square miles land between the valleys of the Tigris and the Euphrates rivers in the modern-day Iraq. Sumer is an ancient name for southern Mesopotamia. The Egyptian culture originated along the Nile River. Historians have found a variety of connections between the Egyptian and Sumer civilizations.

The Indic civilization was shaped, according to Western experts, in the Indus River Valley around the areas called Harappa and Mohenjo-Daro. It is believed that Sumer and Egypt antedated the Indic civilization. Following the Indic civilization, a new civilization emerged in the Aegean islands of Greece. The center of this civilization, called the Minoan, was the largest Aegean island, Crete.

The Chinese civilization started later than the Indic civilization, around the Yangtze and the Hwang-Ho or Yellow rivers. Until the Spanish arrived at the end of the fifteenth century, the Americas had been cut off from the rest of the world. However, around 1500 BC the Mesoamerican civilization had emerged in the Americas, encompassing the Yucatan (Mexico), Guatemala, and Honduras.

Ancient India

The old Western view of the beginning of Indic civilization about 2500 BC has been extended to about 3100 BC around Harappa and Mohenjo-Daro. But based on archeological discoveries, Indic scholars have established the dawn of the Indic civilization to 8000 BC, much earlier than the Mesopotamia or Egyptian civilizations. Accordingly, the Indic civilization may be classified into four prehistoric eras:

(a) Mehrgarh Era (around 8000 BC)
(b) Sarasvati Era (around 7000 BC)
(c) Harappan and Mohenjo-Daro Era (around 3000 BC)
(d) Gangetic Era (around 1000 BC)

The above classification brings us to the beginning of historical times of Lord Mahavira (599 BC–527 BC) and Lord Buddha (563–483 BC) with reasonably well-established dates.

Mehrgarh Era (around 8000 BC)
The town of Mehrgarh was located at the foot of the Bolan Pass in the Baluchistan region. Excavations show that Mehrgarh was a flourishing center of innovation and creativity, placing it in the same league as Jericho. The Mehrgarh people domesticated cattle, grew food, made pottery, and engaged in the exportation and importation of goods.

Sarasvati Era (around 7000 BC)
The discovery of Harappa and Mohenjo-Daro encouraged archeologists to search for other sites along the Indus River. They discovered a number of settlements named Chanhu Daro, Amri, and Kot Diji, and considered them to be a part of Harappa and Mohenjo-Daro, or the Indus Civilization. Later on, the discovery of many more sites which were located in the middle of the desert, away from the Indus River, raised the question: how could the

vanished towns have survived in the midst of a desert? Further research, based on satellite photographs, established that the current Great Indian Desert, or the Thar Desert, was once a great river with fertile banks. Scholars have identified the moribund river as the Sarasvati River. It flowed from the Tibetan part of the Himalayas into the Arabian Sea through the Rajasthan desert, covering a distance almost similar to the Indus River. The Sarasvati River was larger than the Indus River and had been mentioned in the Vedic scriptures. It is believed that the present-day Yamuna River was one of the Sarasvati's main tributaries, which now flows into the Ganges River. The demise of the Sarasvati River is attributed to volcanic eruptions around 2000 BC, during which the earth buckled with sufficient force. This had a devastating effect on the Sarasvati Civilization.

Harappan and Mohenjo-Daro Era (around 3000 BC)
Based on archeological excavations, the Harappan and Mohenjo-Daro civilizations existed along the Indus River. The two urban centers at Harappa and Mohenjo-Daro (now in Pakistan) were well developed with rich agricultural tracts, brick houses, cattle rearing, pottery making, and trade. The citizens of the cities were Austrics and Dravidians. The Austrics migrated from the Mediterranean region while the Dravidians were the original inhabitants. These groups freely mixed, racially and linguistically. The modern descendants of the Austrics are found mainly in central and eastern India, while the Dravidians formed a major segment in southern India.

Both the Sarasvati civilization and the Harappan and Mohenjo-Daro civilization existed together from about 3100 BC until about 2000 BC, although the former flourished for a longer period, almost 4,000 years. The dual civilizations, as mentioned earlier, completely vanished around 2000 BC due to ecological disasters. While the Sarasvati River was converted into a great desert, the course of the Indus River was diverted, leading to massive floods.

Gangetic Era (around 1000 BC)

After the fall of the Sarasvati and Harappan and Mohenjo-Daro civilizations, a new civilization developed around the Ganges River. According to Western historians, this new civilization consisted of Indo-Aryans, who moved into India from east-central Europe. They swept into northwest India in several waves over centuries, using their superior weapons and horse-drawn chariots to subdue the natives and occupy the Ganges region. Supposedly, they established the Vedic culture.

The Aryan-invasion theory was strongly propounded by British scholars arguing that the north Indian Aryans had been different people than the southern Indian Dravidians. Modern India scholars, however, claim that differentiating northern Indians from southern Indians was politically motivated propaganda adopted by the British to divide the Indians in the two regions of the sub-continent. Thus, it has been said that the so-called Aryans and the so-called Dravidians belong to the same Mediterranean branch of the Caucasian race. The people in the South have, comparatively speaking, darker skin than the northerners because the former lived closer to the equator. Besides, there was no archaeological evidence for any significant migrations into India during the post-Sarasvati and post-Harappan-Mohenjo-Daro eras. The Aryan-invasion theory has become a historical fiction.

The Western view that Vedic culture, which is a foundation of the Hindu religion, was developed and inspired by the Aryan invaders, is no longer tenable. Feuerstein, Kak, and Frawley note[6]:

Today we must consider the Vedic peoples as an integral part of the early Indic civilization. They walked the streets of Mohenjo-Daro and Harappa, if not old Mergargh, and had their businesses there and in other towns and villages along the Sarasvati and Indus Rivers and their many tributaries. It is even quite likely that they were principal creators and sustainers of the Indus-Sarasvati civilization.

According to the recent work on the Indic civilization, it appears that the disappearance of the Sarasvati River and the devastation in the Indus region led people to migrate east toward the fertile valley of the Ganges and its tributaries. People moved through thick forests and swamps created by heavy monsoon rains to build a new life for themselves. People who were left behind in the Sarasvati River and the Indus River regions never were able to bounce back by reconstructing a new urban civilization. Instead the center of the Indic civilization shifted from west to east, from the Sarasvati and Indus regions to the Ganges

---

6   *George Feuerstein, Subhash Kak and David Frawley. In Search of the Civilization, Wheaton, IL: Quest Books, 2001.*

region. Thus, a new civilization emerged in the Ganges area around 1000 BC.

Middle-age India

During the Gangetic Era, the entire region was divided into self-contained kingdoms. Each kingdom supported its own military to protect it from outside invasion. The middle-age part of Indian history is organized under the following headings:

(a) Kingdom of Magadha (500 BC–200 BC)
(b) Regional Kingdoms (200 BC–500 AD)
(c) Harsha Period (500 AD–650 AD)
(d) Regional Feudal Kingdoms (650 AD–1000 AD)

Kingdom of Magadha (500BC-200BC)

From 500 BC to 322 BC, the Kingdom of Magadha, which was militarily stronger than others, absorbed its neighbors. It gained dominance over most of north India as it conquered its three most powerful rivals. Historically, the most important Magadha rulers, commonly identified as the Mauryan Empire, were Chandragupta Maurya (322 BC–298 BC) and his grandson, Ashoka (269 BC–232 BC). Chandragupta Maurya, with help of his prime minister Kautilya (author of an ancient book on political administration, which is currently available in English, called *Arthashastra*), created an efficient, centralized bureaucratic government and steadily enlarged his army. At one time, his empire stretched from central Afghanistan to the Bay of Bengal.

During Chandragupta's time, a number of Persian tribes tried to occupy northwest regions of India but were beaten back. In the same era, Alexander the Great led his army to conquer some northern parts of India. But he decided to leave India after his initial victories, leaving little influence on Indian culture. Chandragupta is said to have spent his last days in the company of Jain priests, ritually starving himself to death in a retreat near Mysore.

Chandragupta's son Bindusara (298 BC–273 BC) extended his empire by occupying areas in the South. His son Ashoka penetrated the Bihar, Orissa and the rest of the land and sea routes to both in the East and the West. Under him, the subcontinent acquired a political unity not matched in extent throughout the history of India.

Ashoka fought vigorously in various wars which involved mass killings and bloodshed. But the Kalinga War, fought in the current state of Orissa, changed his life completely. He adopted Buddhism and stopped all political ambitions that involved taking human life. Subsequently, he preached nonviolence and took steps to make the lives of his subjects peaceful and content.

The most remarkable consequence of Ashoka's rule was thought to be the recommendations he made to his subjects in the rock inscriptions and pillars dating from his time, which amounted to a completely new social philosophy. Asoka's precepts are called *Dharma*, a variant of a Sanskrit word meaning "universal law," and their novelty has led to much admiration of Ashoka's modernity by Indian politicians after independence from the British rule in 1947. Ashoka's ideas are striking. He enjoyed respect for the dignity of all men, and, above all, religious toleration and nonviolence. His precepts were general rather than precise; they were not laws. But their central themes are unmistakable and were intended to provide principles of action. They could be considered as a device of government for a huge, heterogeneous and religiously divided empire. The Mauryan Era is considered to be the golden period of Indic history.

Regional Kingdoms (200 BC–500 AD)

The enlightened rule of Ashoka became a model for an ideal king. But without Kautilyan statecraft, neglect of the armed forces and a rivalry between Ashoka's two grandsons seriously undermined the imperial unity and ultimately led to the collapse of the empire in the next fifty years. Different territories split and were occupied by elites who fought each other. For 700 years, India remained a politically fragmented nation, vulnerable to outside invaders.

Harsha Period (500 AD–650 AD)

As mentioned above, after the collapse of the Gupta Empire, regional kingdoms emerged: some small and some large in terms of occupied territory, military strength, and wealth. One of these kingdoms was called Pushyabhuti. Harsha, who became the ruler of the Pushyabhuti in 606 AD, made a determined effort to conquer and unite the entire Indian peninsula. He did capture north India, but failed to subdue the South. After his death, India split into numerous warring regions. King Harsha is noted for his great interest in Sanskrit literature. It is during his time that Kalidasa, the most revered writer of India, lived. One of his books, *The Meghaduta* (The Cloud Messenger) reaches the height of his powers of expression. His descriptions of nature and the fresh and sensual lyricism of his love-poetry are unmatched by poets of any other land or time. In it, the writer relates the story of an exile who asks a cloud to carry a message to his wife. It is not only one of the world's great love-poems, but also a revealing expression of Indian culture and religion.

Regional Feudal Kingdoms (650 AD–1000 AD)

Following the death of the Harsha, India entered a period of political disunity for 400 years. During this period, five political regions emerged:

(a) Ganges River Valley, an area with the city of Kannauj as the center
(b) Ganges Delta, a large territory surrounding today's Bangladesh
(c) Indus Valley, the northwest parts of India
(d) Northwestern Deccan (South)
(e) Southeast Coast of India

Each region was ruled by a succession of dynasties, all with complex histories.

Islamic Rule

Islam had come to India beginning with the Arab traders in the eighth century. Initially, Islamic armies came to India to raid, not to stay. However, in the eleventh century, Turkish Moslems entered India with a different agenda: to make a new home for themselves. The Islamic rule in India is examined in the following categories:

(a) Mahmud of Ghazni (1000 AD–1173 AD)
(b) Muhammad of Ghur (1173 AD–1206 AD)

(c) Sultante of Delhi (1206 AD–1526 AD)

(d) Mughal Dynasty (1526 AD–1858 AD)

Mahmud of Ghazni (1000 AD–1173 AD)

About 1000 AD, Muslims of Iran considered India a prime target for conquest. Mahmud of Ghazni, the son of a Turkish slave-soldier, became the warlord of Afghanistan and Iran and led his armies into India to capture much of the Indus and Ganges regions. Ghanzi is known for devastating northern India, fanatically plundering Hindu, Jain, and Buddhist temples, and looting India's abundant wealth. For example, in the temple of Somnath in 1025, he is said to have taken twenty million gold coins amounting to nearly six and a half tons of gold. His depredations created an economic crisis in India.

Following his death, Mahmud's kingdom fell into disarray and Islamic intervention in northern India slowed for nearly a century. At that time, the Hindu kingdoms of India were able to restore their power and wealth, but squandered much of their resources in battling each other. Although Mahmud's invasion brought no lasting Islamic conquests in India, his invasion tapped the strength of the Hindu kingdoms. While bringing wealth to the Muslims of eastern Iran, Mahmud made the way for later Muslim conquest of India.

Muhammad of Ghur (1173 AD–1206 AD)

In the twelfth century Muhammad of Ghur, a Turkish Muslim, made his first raid into India. Unlike his predecessor, Muhammad strove for permanent conquest of India rather than conquering India to plunder its wealth and retreating back to Afghanistan.

After defeating the Rajput king Prithviraja, near Delhi, he controlled Ganges River Valley and the Ganges River Delta. Thus, he established Islamic rule over all of northern India, with Delhi as his capital.

Sultante of Delhi (1206 AD–1526 AD)

After the death of Muhammad, there followed the Sultante of Delhi, with different military commanders claiming leadership from time to time. It was a time of political upheaval with no one individual acclaimed as the leader on a permanent basis. But Islam had been deeply rooted into Indian society. The Hindu system of government was replaced by Islamic administrative and feudal practices. Millions of Muslims migrated into India, fleeing from neighboring countries, and millions of Hindus were converted to Islam. Almost one-quarter of the subcontinent's population at that time consisted of Muslims.

The first rulers of Islamic India were Mamluks (military slaves), who captured power upon their master's death. After that, other military commanders maintained control of the country until replaced by a stronger commander. Historically, among the different sultanate of Delhi, the names of Ala al-Din Khalji and Muhammad ibn Tughluq stand out. They kept on fighting the Hindu kingdoms in order to spread their influence as far as possible. By 1335 Muhammad ibn Tughluq had won all of India except the southern tip.

Mughal Dynasty (1526 AD–1858 AD)

In the early sixteenth century, a new Afghan commander named Babur invaded India and crushed the army of the sultante of Delhi. By his death in 1530, Babur had captured most of north India and founded the Mughal dynasty, which dominated India for the next two hundred years.

The Mughal had to fight the local Indian Muslims as well as the Hindus to maintain control. After Babur, his son Hamayu ruled India and was followed by Akbar, who is held to be a great king for a variety of reasons. In his 63 years (1542 AD–1605 AD), Akbar subdued all of northern India and Afghanistan and created a centralized administration and modern army. He implemented land reform to provide peasants their fair share. He went out of his way to unite Muslims and Hindus in a new society with a new religion that was to be called Divine Faith, with himself as the high priest; but neither Hindus nor Muslims accepted his views.

Akbar's son Jahangir and his grandson, Shah Jahan, continued to rule India without any significant events. However, Shah Jahan had a great interest in building grand structures and monuments. His greatest legacy to the world is the Taj Mahal, which he built in memory of his beloved wife, Mumtaz. The Taj Mahal was completed in 1634.

Up until the time that Shah Jahan ruled India, almost one hundred years following Akbar's death, Islamic culture had reached its highest form. Nearly all of India was united into a single prosperous state and Islamic arts flourished.

While Shah Jahan was still alive, his sons fought each other to become the ruler. His younger son Aurangzeb killed his three brothers and imprisoned his father and became emperor. His tyranny, oppressive taxes, and failed conquests ultimately led to the collapse of the Mughal dynasty. This sparked massive rebellions of the Rajputs (residents of the present state of Rajastan), Sikhs, and Marathas (residents of the present state of Maharashtra) under their leader Shivaji. By the eighteenth century, India was again in political chaos and was ripe for eventual conquest by the British. Mughal emperors continued to rule at Delhi as powerless puppets until the last ruler was finally deposed by the British in 1858.

British in India

The first European intervention in India involved the establishment of Portuguese trading colonies in 1498 and the Portuguese acquisition of the port of Goa in 1510. Thereafter, the Dutch conquered Ceylon (modern Sri Lanka), while the French and British established control over important ports such as Madras, Bombay, and Calcutta. The British rule in India may be summarized under the following headings:

(a) East India Company
(b) British Conquest of India
(c) Effects of British Rule
(d) Indian Nationalism

East India Company

It was not until the collapse of the effective power of the Mughal emperors in the mid-eighteenth century that the Europeans became major players on the Indian scene.

The earliest British involvement in India was not an official government act, but an effort by the British East India Company seeking purely economic gain. The goal of the British (and other European nations) was not military conquest but the establishment of ports and the control of trade and industry. However, they were not averse to using military force and Indian mercenary armies to accomplish these goals.

British Conquest of India

From 1756 to 1763, British and French forces clashed in Europe, North America, West Africa, and India. In India, British forces, along with their Indian allies, met the French and their allies at the Battle of Plessey in 1757, which ended in a decisive victory for the British, laying the foundation for creation of the British Empire in India. Thereafter, the British increasingly adopted a policy of territorial expansion in India as the means to ensure their economic supremacy. During the next century, all of India was conquered or otherwise acquired by the British. India has been considered the most important European colonial possession in the Afro-Asian world.

Effects of British Rule

British rule in India had mixed results. On the one hand, the British managed to bring political order and economic stability to the subcontinent as they played the unbiased outsider and brought a temporary end to sectarian and ethnic differences between Hindus and Muslims. A great deal of modernization also occurred with the introduction of railways, telegraphing, and other western technologies. Many Indians received western education, which enabled them to adopt modern technologies, methods, and procedures in their country.

On the other hand, there were numerous problems with British rule in India. In a sense, the British people became a new Indian "caste," occupying the most privileged and powerful positions in Indian society, while forcing the natives to serve as subordinates. Further, although the British did a lot to modernize India, most economic benefits accrued to the British. British policies were not designed to create much love on the part of the Indians. Since people of Indian origin were excluded from senior government positions, the social and economic gap between British overlords and Indians widened. For example, in the interest of promoting British goods, the British refused to allow large-scale industrial development in India. Such mercantilist policies exacerbated large-scale poverty in the country.

The native dissatisfaction with British rule in India culminated in 1857 with the unsuccessful Indian uprising led by the army of subordinates (sepoys) called the Sepoy Rebellion. The rebellion was crushed. The crown subsequently took over most of the functions of the East India Company and thus imposed imperial rule in India.

After 1858, India's 300 million people were governed by an elite British civil service. This administrative core was supported by a military force consisting of British officers and Indian troops. The rules and procedures were enforced in such a way that Indians remained second-class citizens in their own country. Such elitism and racism were hardly conducive to warm relations.

In sum, despite the relative benevolence of the British rule, it was still a case of a foreign power dominating the native peoples. By the late nineteenth century a new generation of Indian intellectuals, trained in western colleges, but still loyal to their homeland and traditions, began the long process which ultimately led to India's independence after World War II.

Indian Nationalism

It was inevitable that nationalist sentiments should find expression in India, though these were expressed in different ways. The Indian National Congress, founded in 1855, expressed faith in the ability of the Indians to work with the British in a gradual process of reform, eventually leading toward independence. Mohandas Karamchand Gandhi was the principal adherent of this nonviolent and peaceful strategy that sought to win India's independence from the British. Jawaharlal Nehru, independent India's first prime minister, was a core adherent of the nonviolent view. Subhash Chandra Bose, another national leader, supported forcefully gaining India's freedom through military confrontation with the British. B.G. Tilk favored militant nationalism that was not only anti-British but also anti-Muslim. In the end, Gandhi's nonviolent actions found wide acceptance among Indian intellectuals and the common man.

Independent India

The British, in principal, agreed to free India after the Second World War as long as the Indian leadership supported the British in wartime. The Indians agreed to this arrangement. At the end of the war, Indian independence became a major issue for the British. As they were still contemplating freeing India, Indian Muslims, fearing Hindu domination in the new independent state, began to voice a strong desire for a separate Muslim state. Gandhi strongly opposed partition of India on religious grounds, but his view did not hold sway. In 1947, the British government passed the India Independence Act, partitioning the country into two separate states, India and Pakistan.

Pakistan became a fully Muslim state in 1947 with millions of Hindus migrating to "new" India from the territories which became a part of Pakistan. India, at the outset, declared itself to be a secular state and gave the option to the Muslims within its boundaries to stay in India or migrate to Pakistan. Many million Muslims left India while millions stayed back.

Mohandas K. Gandhi, in reverence called Mahatma Gandhi by Indians, was never comfortable with the partition of India and hoped instead for a state in which Hindus and Muslims could live together in peace. Unfortunately for the Mahatma, his dream was overwhelmed by the reality of religious and political strife. Unhappy at the partition, he continued to call for tolerance toward Muslims in India. But on January 30, 1948, just a few months after one of Gandhi's dreams—Indian independence—had been realized, he was gunned down by a Hindu religious fanatic.

Indian Republic

On January 26, 1950, India became a constitutional democracy with the president as the head of the country and the prime minister as the head of the government, with two houses of elected members, the lower house (similar to the U.S. House of Representatives) and the upper house (similar to the U.S. Senate). The leader of the majority party in the lower house becomes the prime minister. India's constitution combines British traditions, American experiences, and her own values. Dr. B.R. Ambedkar, a member of India's untouchable caste, played a key role in drafting the constitution.

Modern India

India's journey since independence has seen its share of ups and downs. The country has experienced a saga of fledging population and scarce resources, including food. But as we enter the twenty-first century, the country has come a long way. India's is a tale of amazing resilience and patience. It has emerged as a globally dominant knowledge economy showing grit and determination against the odds. As we look to the future, in 2040 India is expected to be the third largest economy in the world, behind China and the United States.

Today, India is a pluralistic society of over one billion people. It is an enigma, a country of contrasts. On the one hand, in 2010, it is the fifth largest industrial power in the world, and, on the other hand, it is the twelfth poorest nation in per capita terms. From possessing the second largest pool of scientific and technical manpower, it has the dubious distinction of having the largest number of illiterates in the world. While it possesses formidable nuclear capability, it struggles with basic metallurgy to produce a needle of consistent quality. Metropolitan and urban India presents a picture of an affluent minority enjoying hedonistic lifestyles. It coexists with the grinding poverty of rural India that possesses its own mosaic of light and shade. Whatever horizon one may paint, the enduring reality of two Indias is apparent.

India, a great steaming stew of diverse nationalities, religions, and languages, is in fact much more a continent than a country. Geographically, the large, tri-angular-shaped nation is separated from the rest of Asia mainly by the Himalayan Mountains. The Republic of India, called Bharat in native languages, has an area of 1,269,346 square miles (3,287,593 kilometers), less than one-half that of the United States. It has a warm climate, dominated by the seasonal winds known as monsoons. However, because of its size, relief, extremes of elevation, and relation to the oceans, it has many local variations of temperature and rainfall.

In 2010, about 45 percent of the population of India lived in urban areas (about 2,500 towns and cities), an increase of ten percent since 1947. The remaining 55 percent lived in more than 500,000 villages. The drift to the urban areas is obviously revolutionary in its effects on Indian life. Many urban dwellers maintain their ties with village life. They take back to their villages new ideas of what is possible and desirable, and the villages themselves change, though slowly. Increasingly, among the mud huts of the drier areas or the thatched cottages of the deltas, there are small brick buildings—local administrative or welfare offices, but most of all, schools. The literacy rate lags in rural areas and among women, but for all of India, it rose from 14 percent of the population in 1947 to 60 percent in 2010.

India is the birthplace of Hinduism, Buddhism, Jainism, and Sikhism. As a secular state, however, India has no official religion, and religious toleration is guaranteed under the constitution. Hindus constitute about 80 percent of the population, Muslims 13 percent, Christians three percent, Sikhs two percent, Jains 1.5 percent, Buddhists one percent, and Zoroastrians a few hundred thousand.

The caste system, a set of social and occupational classes into which individuals are born, is an important facet of Hinduism and thus is a dominant feature of Indian life. Since independence, the government has attempted to eliminate castes, but caste consciousness remains important in Indian politics, despite the fact that such discrimination is unconstitutional. Harijans, the lowest caste, traditionally called the untouchables, who constitute 15 percent of the population, and tribes who constitute seven percent, are given special protection by the federal government.

About 200 different languages are spoken in India and an appreciation of the linguistic divisions provides a key to better understanding of the nation. Four principle language groups are recognized, of which Hindi and Dravidian are the most important. Hindi is the official language; English is also widely used in government and business. In addition, thirteen other languages have received official recognition in the constitution: Assamese, Bengali, Gujarati, Kashmiri, Marathi, Oriya, Punjabi, Sindhi, Urdu, Kannada, Malayalam, Tamil, and Telugu. Sanskrit provides the root for many of the Indian languages but is no longer a spoken language. Many other languages are spoken by smaller groups; these are either regional variations or dialects.

If diversity is the most conspicuous feature of India, ineffable strands of unity are nonetheless unmistakable and give India a continuity of culture and persistence of traits in its long time span. Indians value physical purity and refinement of spirit highly. Acceptance of day-to-day living incidents as will of Fate (or God) is widespread as is the idea of Karmas (past deeds during the present birth or in previous births). Many urbanized women are liberated, but modesty and shyness are traditionally valued in women. Social harmony is important: an Indian will say yes to a request than risk upsetting someone by saying no.

The basic social unit in India is the family, which takes precedence over the individual. In most families, aunts, uncles, and other relatives live together, although this trait is dying out as young professionals move to towns and cities and away from their families.

Vedic Philosophy

Perhaps the most basic aspect of Indic civilization is the Vedic philosophy. The Vedic philosophy had been the basis of what later on began to be called Vedic religion. The modern-day Hinduism, the religion of 80 percent of India's people, is derived from the Vedic religion. Before reviewing the Vedic philosophy, two points should be made clear.

First is the antiquity of the Vedic culture. According to western historians, Vedic philosophy was given to India by the invading tribe or Aryans who supposedly migrated to India from Asian Minor and destroyed the Harappan and Mohenjo-Daro culture. But as mentioned earlier, the Western view of the Aryan invasion has been totally rejected by new archeological discoveries. Indian scholars believe that the Vedic philosophy originated during the Sarasvati era (around 6000 BC) if not earlier. It is because there has been evidence of Vedic views during the Sarasvati era, as determined from the excavations in the region of the now-vanished Sarasvati River. Further, seals have been found in the Harappan and Mohenjo-Daro excavations that refer to the Vedic perspective. Briefly, the philosophy is much older than what Western scholars lead us to believe.

Second, there is the question of whether there were any other philosophies prominent in prehistoric India. Jain scholars believe that Jainism is the oldest religion of the world, and base their argument on excavations found in the Sarasvati and Harappan-Mohenjo-Daro regions. The seals from these eras show the first Jain Tirthankara, Lord Adinatha, was revered and worshipped then.

It might be that the Jain sect and the Vedic philosophy originated sometime during the Sarasvati, era simultaneously. The Jain principles requiring extreme asceticism did not have as much following as the Vedic philosophy, which became more popular. The Vedic principles were more practical for humans to follow and thus they spread among the large majority quickly. Today, both Jainism and Hinduism continue to be practiced side by side. But while there are over 800 million Hindus, the number of Jains is about 1.5 percent of India's present-day population of over one billion people.

The Vedic philosophy is examined under the following headings:

(a) Vedic Religion
(b) Brahmanism
(c) Hinduism
(d) Vedic and Hindu Literature
(e) The Meaning of Life Literature: The Vedas
(f) The Ritual Literature: The Brahmanas and the Aranyakas
(g) The Esoteric Literature: The Upanishads
(h) Post-Vedic Age Literature: The Ramayana and The Bhagavad-Gita
(i) Interpretations and Practices

Vedic Religion

According to Vedic philosophy, gods, humans, and other living beings are the results of the sacrificed creative act of Manu, a superhuman being. The gods are immortals while the humans are mortal, subject to life and death. Humans are weak and cannot defend themselves from demons that threaten the world order. Thus humans must seek protection from gods through pleasing them with worship, sacrificial gifts, and obedience.

The cosmic elements, being subject to depletion over time, require renewal on an ongoing basis. The renewal takes place by absorbing matter and energy from sacrificial victims. Thus, the performance of sacrifices became an important part of the Vedic philosophy.

Although there are countless gods and goddesses, 33 gods were considered major deities, eleven for each sphere (heaven, earth, and hell). Gods adopted various human forms and personified such natural forces as the sun, the moon, fire and plants. The Vedic gods, born after the creation of the world, lived peacefully and harmoniously. Mostly males, they dressed and ate like humans, and entertained themselves with music and gambling and drank a hallucinatory drink called *Soma* that gave them immorality. Collectively, governed by the nature, they forced the mortal humans to comply with orders promulgated by them. They rewarded those who respected them, punished those who ignored them. They frequently fought the demons to protect the universe from evil.

Brahmanism

In the initial stages of the Vedic religion, the sacrificial offerings involved only the sacrifices and the god which could be held at home. As years went by, the priests introduced ritualistic complexities in sacrificial ceremonies that necessitated their involvement to conduct them.

About 1000 to 500 BC, the priests transformed the Vedic religion into a rationalized system of sacrifice, often called Brahmanism. Brahmanism downplayed the role of gods by emphasizing the direct connection between humans and nature. It emphasized the central role of priests in integrating the humans into the mainstream of religious thought. They assured the devotees that rewards were automatic, provided sacrifices adhered to the right rituals. This made the priests powerful.

The priests, called the Brahmins in Sanskrit, became an elite class, requiring rulers and common men alike to depend on them for living happy and moralistic lives. Often, they engaged in unethical behavior for personal gain. Some reform-minded intellectuals and ascetics questioned the thesis propounded by Brahmanism, and the collective opinions of these reformers marked the end of Brahmanism. It was at that time, about 400 BC, that Hinduism began to take shape.

Hinduism

Initially, in its evolution, 400 BC to 200 BC, Hinduism retained many traditional features of Brahmanism, such as sacrifices and the worship of ancient Vedic gods. But these features were eventually abandoned and replaced by a triumvirate philosophy during the Mauryan period.

Following this philosophy, Hindus believe in one god who could be called Brahma, the creator; Vishnu, the pre-server; and Shiva, the destroyer of the universe. The concept of a triumvirate continues to be the guiding principle of Hinduism today. Most worshipped among the three supreme beings has been Vishnu, who keeps the cosmos order functioning properly. The literature identifies Vishnu by 1001 names. In different parts of India, Vishnu is worshipped by various names. The Hindu god is neither male nor female, yet Hindus consider god as a pair—a male and a female. According to Hinduism, God gives us life, sustains us, and absorbs us back into himself or sends us back to earth in the form of a new life.

- <u>God as a Giver:</u> He is called *Brahma* and has with him *Sarasvati,* who has the power to grant wisdom.
- <u>God as a Sustainer:</u> He is called *Vishnu* and has with him *Lakshmi,* who has the power to grant wealth.
- <u>God as an Aborber:</u> He is called *Shiva* or *Mahesh* and has with him *Durga,* or *Kali,* who has the power to grant physical strength.

Briefly, when Hindus remember god as a giver of life, he is Brahma; as a sustainer of life, he is Vishnu; and the god that dissolves life is called Shiva or Mahesh. God as a granter of wisdom is Sarasvati, as a granter of wealth and prosperity is Lakshmi and as a granter of strength is Durga or Kali. Likewise, Hindus call the god by different names depending on what one is seeking. For example, god as a remover of obstacles is called Ganapati.

Hindus believe that god Vishnu, the sustainer of life, from time to time appears in human form to wipe out evil. For example, Lord Rama and Lord Krishna were the incarnations of Vishnu as the perfect souls on earth.

The word *Om,* which is sacred to Hindus, means "yes." It is recited before and after every prayer. Similarly, the symbol of the swastika is considered sacred. It means "may all be well with you." The symbol is marked on walls, floors, and other places, for auspiciousness.

Hinduism is a flexible religion. Its ability to assimilate competing ideologies and practices enabled it to accept all religions as valid approaches for seeking truth and living happily. Hindus have accommodated the intellectual and spiritual ideas and practices of its diverse sects of believers such as Jains, Muslims, Sikhs, Buddhists, Christians, Zoroastrians, Jews, and others. Doctrinal flexibility provided Hinduism the capacity to absorb rival religions, to tolerate the growth and spread of secularism within its own ranks, and to secure and retain the loyalty of India's illiterate masses through assimilation of popular folk arts, deities, and devotional practices.

It is important to recognize that Hinduism does not follow a linear progression from a founder through an organizational system with sects branching off from it. Rather, it is the mosaic of distinct cults, deities, sects, and ideas duly adjusted to emerging beliefs and socioeconomic realities. An individual is a constituent part of the world soul. It seeks to free itself from the mortal cycle. This requires going through a series of birth-death cycles until the Karmas (the deeds and conduct) are good enough for the release.

Over time, the intellectuals and teachers redefined, expanded, and consolidated traditional values and beliefs of Hinduism to a new religious and social complex. It provided the practitioners an integrative philosophy of a hierarchical social organization. As it evolved, it included select teachings from Upanishads (discussed below), reaffirmed essential doctrines from the Vedic religion, and paid attention to folk traditions and basic tenets of other religions.

Vedic and the Hindu Literature

The Vedic and Hindu scriptures and literature consist of hundreds of books. For basic insights, the literature may be divided into three categories as illustrated in Exhibit A:

(a) Vedic-Age literature, which consists of the four Vedas and the Brahmanas.
(b) Post-Vedic literature comprising Aranyakas and Upanishads, the Ramayana and the Bhagavad-Gita.
(c) Interpretations and practices.

Exhibit A
Major Categories of Vedic and Hindu Scriptures

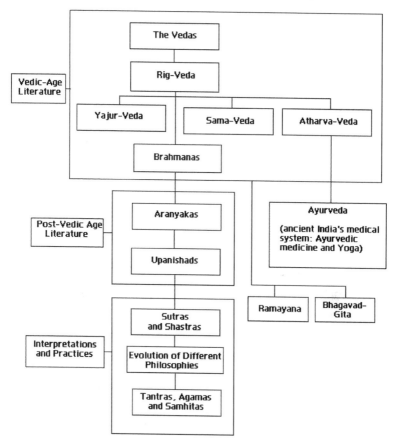

The Vedas

The Vedas, (also called the Puranas, or wisdom books), are the oldest and most revered scriptures of Indic civilization. They comprise ancient knowledge and consist of four compilations: the *Rig-Veda*, the *Yajur-Veda*, the *Sama-Veda*, and the *Atharva-Veda*. These scriptures contain invocations, prayers, detailed rituals, and philosophical treatises. The oldest among them is the *Rig-Veda*, which was composed between 5000-4000 BC. The other three Vedas were composed almost a millennium later.

The focus of the Vedas is on providing contentment, courage, energy, fearlessness, forgiveness, mercy, good life, happiness, health, intellect, long life, mental growth, mercy, peace, progeny, prosperity, purification, reward for virtue, righteousness, freedom from sin, success in general, achievement in business, victory, wealth, welfare, wisdom and zeal. Most of the verses are in the form of direct or indirect prayers. They convey moral instruction on how God wants humans to live their lives in order to be happy and content in the universe he created. Overall, the Vedas show poetic sophistication and spiritual depth. Here are further details of the four Vedas:

- *Rig-Veda*: Basic wisdom comprising 1,028 hymns and 10,589 verses organized in ten chapters.
- *Sama-Veda*: Liturgical manual for reading and singing the Vedic hymns comprising 1,875 stanzas from the *Rig-Veda* and about 75 additional verses.
- *Yajur-Veda*: It consists of hymns for sacrificial rituals or prayers. More than one-third of its approximately 2,000 verses, organized in more than 40 chapters, are taken from the *Rig-Veda*. The remaining third are original to the *Yajur-Veda*.

- *Atharva-Veda*: It includes hymns, or prayers for health-related remedies. Organized into 23 chapters, it has almost 6,000 verses of which about 20 percent are drawn from the *Rig-Veda*.

Overall, the *Rig-Veda* focuses on sacred utterances; the *Sama-Veda* concentrates on sacred songs and/or inner meanings of the utterances; the *Yajur-Veda* specifies ritual methods and procedures; and the *Atharva-Veda* represents words as power.

Mention must be made of two modern aspects of *Atharva-Veda*. These are *ayurvedic* medicine and *yoga*. *Atharva-Veda* includes many hymns for the purpose of healing. These hymns formed the basis of the evolution of ayurvedic medicine, which even in today's India is popularly practiced.

In the West, yoga has been understood and practiced in a narrow sense. It is considered as a system to promote physical and mental well-being, or *hatha* yoga, comprising physical exercises and postures, breathing techniques, and meditation. Yoga, it has been claimed, provides a balanced and wholesome approach to achieving perfect physical and mental health, happiness, and tranquility.

In India, yoga has much deeper meaning. It symbolizes India's spirituality, and the practice of yoga facilitates spiritual awakening. Yoga's roots date back to Vedic times.

The Sanskrit word yoga translates as the union between body, mind, and spirit which is the route to achieving higher paths or *Moksha*. Professor Abraham Kaplan explains this sublime ideal in the following words[7]:

---

7   Abraham Kaplan, _The New World of Philosophy_. New York: Vintage Books, 1961, pp. 227-228.

The goal of moksha, of emancipation, though individual in form (like the Western quest for personal salvation), is thoroughly social in content. In a way, it goes beyond even the prevailing Western conception of moving from egoism to altruism. For the goal is not unselfishness but selflessness, a movement, not from self to other, but from self to self, in which there is no other.

Although in day-to-day life, individuals deviate from the path of spirituality, India's social structure is intertwined with spiritual values. To illustrate the point, the Hindu philosophy prescribes four human goals: material welfare (*artha*), pleasure which includes aesthetic satisfaction as well as sexual fulfillment (*kama*), morality (*dharma*), and spiritual liberation (*moksha*). Yoga, through the renunciation of the world, leads to inner peace and self-realization, which, according to Indic philosophy, should be the highest goal of an individual. Even in its modern-day adaptation, yoga is useful. It can be practiced by anyone, regardless of age and ability. Its holistic approach provides tools to help one cope with the challenges of daily life.

Although the Vedas are religious texts, they make reference to worldly matters. For example, the Vedas indicate that the Vedic culture spread all over India. Following the Vedic precepts, the area was partitioned into numerous independent tribal kingdoms. The tribes gradually moved from pastoralism to farming and stock breeding. A culture emerged with Sanskrit as its language. Three common institutions took roots among the adherents that persist to the present day. These are: the extended family, the autonomous village, and the caste system.

Extended Family

The society adopted a patriarchal social structure based on the extended family. A close-knit group, the family was ruled by its eldest male. Members' roles and responsibilities varied by age and sex. Youth had to submit to elders and females to males. The collective interests of the family prevailed over those of each individual.

Autonomous Village

Most Vedic people lived in small farming villages, although cities later emerged, developing political, commercial, and military activities. Each village was ruled by a royal appointee, who was responsible for civil, judicial, and military matters. He was assisted by a council consisting of local dignitaries.

Caste System

The society was divided into four social groups called *Brahmins* (priests), *Kshatriyas* (warriors), *Vaishyas* (artisans, merchants, and farmers), and *Sudras* (servants and slaves).

The caste system represents a society founded on a complex structure of mutual obligations and social and religious responsibilities. Unlike the modern day, where law is used primarily to define one's rights, during the Vedic period, the religious law (Dharma) was used to define one's responsibilities and obligations to the gods and humans. Thus, a low-caste person would not feel that his rights were being violated by the limitations of his caste, but would perceive that the gods had given him a different set of responsibilities than those of the high-caste priest or a warrior. It was commonly agreed that society could function only if each individual fulfilled his responsibilities, as defined by his caste.

The Brahmanas and the Aranyakas

The Brahmanas explore the meanings of the Vedic hymns and provide practical guidance for the priests to narrate and sing the hymns. Over time, the Vedic rituals evolved into complexities which people found difficult to handle. This necessitated the use of specialists who could memorize the hymns, their melodies, and the accompanying ritual gestures. It also involved undertaking Vedic sacrificial ceremonies in keeping with the astronomical and calendrical knowledge as propounded in the Vedas.

These specialists came to be known as Brahmins. They emerged as a professional class of hereditary priests for performing the Vedic ceremonies. The Brahmanas are the ritual texts that the Brahmins followed in rendering their services.

The Aranyakas are scriptures that define the ritual obligations of the jungle-dwellers, i.e., those who have fulfilled their householder duties and have moved in solitude into the forest. The jungle-dwellers were supposed to perform more advanced, and potentially more dangerous rituals than the householders. It was through such rituals that they could purify themselves and gain mystical powers. The Aranyakas also include a variety of meditation and devotional teachings.

The Upanishads

The Brahmins became elitist in telling laymen how the Vedic rituals and ceremonies should be performed. They increasingly specified minor details which often became unbearable. Ultimately, the Brahmins' excesses encouraged a small group of reform-minded intellectuals and ascetics within the priest and warrior castes to abandon concentration on rituals and focus their energies on such matters as the nature of the universe, God, and the true self. Through this they aspired to find the means by which the individual soul could secure permanent release from the recurring cycle of birth and death. The philosophical speculations of these reformers are collected in 123 *Upanishads*, marking the end of the Vedic era. It is from them that Hinduism derived its essential tenets.

The Upanishads may be regarded as the metaphysical treatises that are full of sublime conceptions and intuitions of universal truth. The core emphasis of the Upanishads is on self-realization through wisdom.

According to the Upanishads, each individual soul is a constituent part of the world soul. It seeks to free itself from its mortal poison and the wheel of life. To do so, it is forced to undergo a long and painful series of bodily reincarnations and transmigrations. The bodily form that imprisons the soul in each existence is predetermined by deeds and conduct (i.e., karma), perpetrated in the previous life. Upanishad scholars offered three paths for acquiring release and true knowledge: right action and deeds, devotion, and renunciation of the world through an ascetic life. They denied that true knowledge was possible through sensory and empirical means; instead, they urged ascetics to engage in psychic exercises and yoga as a means to induce trance to help achieve unity with the god.

The Ramayana and The Bhagavad-Gita

The *Ramayana* is the life story of Lord Sri Rama, an incarnation of the god Vishnu. He appeared as a human to spread the word of leading a just and peaceful life, and to destroy demon Ravana, the King of Ceylon (present-day Sri Lanka). The story supposedly belongs to the era of about 1500 BC.

The story traces the life of Sri Rama, his wife, Sita, and his brother, Laxshman, as they wander through the forests for fourteen years. He was supposed to become the king of his state, the oldest of the four sons of his father, Dashratha. But his jealous stepmother forced Dashratha to name her own son to be the king and to ask Sri Rama to spend fourteen years away from home. The stepmother had helped Dashratha in a battle and he, at that time, had promised her that she could ask for any favor in return. The stepmother used that promise to force Sri Rama out. It had been the tradition of the family to keep one's word, or promise, even if it meant giving life. So this is what Dashratha did.

While Sri Rama, Sita, and Laxshman were in a dense forest, Ravana kidnapped Sita and brought her to Ceylon, his kingdom. Sri Rama had to kill Ravana to get Sita back. The story narrates what obstacles Sri Rama had to go through to do that. In this endeavor, the monkey-god Hanumana played a key role. Many Hindus even today worship Hanumana.

Incidentally, the day Sri Rama killed the evil king Ravana is celebrated in modern India as the *Dusherra* festival. After killing Ravana, it took Sri Rama twenty days to return to his kingdom city, Ayodhaya. Thus, twenty days after *Dusherra*,

Hindus (as well as other religious groups, for different reasons) celebrate *Diwali*, often called the Festival of Lights, or Deepawali. It is the most important festival of India.

The *Bhagavad-Gita* is a holy dialogue between Lord Krishna, another incarnation of god Vishnu, and a prince named Arjuna. Arjuna had to launch a battle against his evil stepbrothers. But he was having second thoughts about whether it was right to kill his own kin just for the sake of capturing the kingdom.

It is on the battlefield that Sri Krishna explains to Arjuna his duty as a person and his relationship with God. The sermon was delivered by Sri Krishna to Arjuna about 1100 BC.

The *Gita* shows how to overcome your weakness and perform your duties. By doing so, a man can live a contented and joyful life. It also explains the purpose of man on this earth and helps humans to discover God in their own hearts. Through following the commandments of Sri Krishna, as elaborated in the *Gita*, we can achieve success, happiness, and salvation. The *Gita* is probably the most revered book among the Hindus. Its message has the power of changing a person's life completely by its ability to infuse the spirit of humility toward God and humans.

The *Gita* advises a person to believe in himself or herself and undertake action accordingly. The underlying message of the *Gita* is that a person's job is to do his or her duty and accept the results bravely without getting depressed, that is with a smile and without complaint. The *Gita* emphasizes that a person is given the freedom to pursue the path of virtue or of sin as well as the path of action or of laziness. Each path has its consequences. But the path of virtue and hard work is the path to realize the god and thus derive happiness and peace within and without. Appendix C at the end of this book examines different aspects of the *Gita* in more details.

Interpretations and Practices

Following the Upanishads, different works have been produced that define the rituals, ethics, grammar, etymology, astronomy, etc., of the Vedic and Post-Vedic Age literature. They are called *Sutras* and *Shastras*. In addition, as time passed, different schools of philosophy evolved. The literature of various philosophical systems appeared that explained their approaches, core values, and ways of living as humans. For example, one philosophy concentrated on vegetarianism as a basic principle. Other schools permitted non-vegetarian diet that did not involve killing the mother cow.

Over time, a variety of *tantras*, *agamas*, and *samhitas* were written that provided different ways for humans to live their lives happily. This literature stressed how strength can be gained, how power can be achieved, and how thinking of the other person can be changed.

Conclusion

Today's India is a vast land of over one billion people who live in harmony with nature and with each other, and who have a philosophy dating back to Vedic times. In layman's language this philosophy suggests that you free your heart from hatred, free your mind from worries, live simply, give more, and expect less. India is a truly multicultural society where people with different affiliations and identities are able to live in harmony. As an example, in 2004, the country with a more than 80 percent Hindu population, was led by a Sikh prime minister, Manmohan Singh, and headed by a Muslim president, Abdul Kalam, with the ruling party (Congress) presided over by a Christian woman, Sonia Gandhi. In India such perspectives of multiculturalism are common in different fields, from business to politics and from cinema to sports. Despite occasional episodes of disturbances between people of different religions, castes, and languages, India's people, by and large, are tolerant and peaceful.

Appendix B

The Bhaktamar Stotra

Stotra 1:
When the gods bow down at the feet of Lord Rishabhdeva, the radiance of the jewels of their crowns is intensified by the divine glow of the nails of his feet. The mere touch of his feet absolves the beings from sins. He who prostrates himself at these feet crosses the mundane barriers of rebirth into the state of liberation. I convey my reverential salutations at the feet of Lord Rishabhdeva, the first Tirthankara, and the propagator of religion at the beginning of this era.

Stotra 2:
Celestial lords, with prudence acquired through the true understanding of all the canons, have eulogized Bhagavan Adinatha with hymns captivating the audience in the three realms-heaven, earth, and hell. I, Manatungacharya, a humble man with little wisdom shall also endeavor to eulogize that first Tirthankara.

Stotra 3:
Only an ignorant child attempts an impossible task like grabbing the reflection of the moon in the water. Similarly, O Jina, Out of impudence alone I am trying, in spite of my ignorance, to eulogize you, who have been revered by the gods.

Stotra 4:
O ocean of virtues! Can even Brihaspati, the guru of Gods, with the help of his unlimited wisdom, narrate your virtues pure and blissful as the moon? Can a man swim across the reptile infested ocean in fury, lashed by gales of deluge?

Stotra 5:
O Apostle of apostles! I do not possess the wisdom to narrate your infinite virtues. Still, driven by devotion, I intend to compose a hymn in your praise. It is well known that to protect her fawn, even a doe puts her feet down and faces a lion, forgetting her own frailty. Similarly, devotion impels me to take on the task of composing the hymn without assessing my own capacity.

Stotra 6:
O Embodiment of pure wisdom! I have so little knowledge that I am an object of ridicule for the wise. Still, my devotion for you stirs me to sing hymns in your praise, as the mango blossoms inspire the cuckoo's melodious song.

Stotra 7:
The malignant Karmas accumulated by the living beings are instantly erased by praising you, just as the piercing sun rays dispel the all enveloping dense darkness, as black as a bumble-bee.

Stotra 8:
I compose this panegyric with the belief that, though composed by an ignorant like me, it will certainly please noble people due to your divine influence. Indeed, when on lotus

leaves, dewdrops gleam like pearls, presenting a pleasant sight.

Stotra 9:
The brilliant sun is far away; still, at dawn its soft glow makes the drooping lotus buds bloom. Similarly, O Jina! Let alone the immeasurable powers of your eulogy, the mere utterance of your name with devotion absolves mundane beings of sin and purifies them.

Stotra 10:
O Lord of the living! O Eminence of the world! It is not surprising that he, who is engrossed in praising your infinite virtues, attains your exalted position. It should not be surprising if a benevolent master makes his subjects his equals. In fact, what is the use of serving a master who does not allow his followers to attain an exalted position like his?

Stotra 11:
O Jina! Your divine magnificence is spell-binding. After looking at your divine form nothing else pleases the eye. Who would like to taste seawater after drinking fresh water of the divine ocean of milk, pure and soothing like moonlight?

Stotra 12:
O Crown of the three realms! It appears as if the quiescence and harmony imparting ultimate particles became extinct after constituting your body, because I do not witness elsewhere such out of the world magnificence as yours.

Stotra 13:
Lord! I do not relish comparing your face to the moon. How can your glowing visage, which gods, angels, humans and other beings alike are pleased to behold, be compared with the blemished moon, dull and pale by the day as autumn leaves? Truly, even the best metaphor for your face is inadequate.

Stotra 14:
O Lord of the three realms! Outshining the full moon, your infinite virtues permeate the universe beyond the three realms; hymns extolling your virtues resound all over. Who can restrain the devotees of the only omnipotent one?

Stotra 15:
O dispassionate One! Divine nymphs, through wanton gestures have toiled fruitlessly to distract you, but you have remained unmoved. The doomsday tempest that shakes common hills cannot disturb even the tip of the great Mount Sumeru.

Stotra 16:
Lord! You are the divine lamp that needs neither wick nor oil; whose flame emits no smoke, remains steady even in the storm that moves the immovable, and lights up the three realms.

Stotra 17:
O Monk among monks! Your boundless glory exceeds the suns. The sun passes through cycles of day and night, but the orb of your omniscience shines forever. The sun can be

eclipsed, but your glow eternally lights the whole world. The sun's rays are blocked by mere clouds, but your passionless, infinite, virtuous glory cannot. The sun shines on only part of the world at a time, but nothing can obstruct your radiance.

Stotra 18:
Your lotus face, O Lord, is the moon par excellence. The moon shines only at night and that too in a fortnightly cycle, but your face is ever radiant. The moonlight penetrates darkness only to dimly, but your face removes the universal darkness of ignorance and desire. The moon is eclipsed as well as covered by clouds, but nothing can veil your face.

Stotra 19:
O Lord of the Universe! Where is the need of the sun during the day and the moon during the night when your ever-radiant face sweeps away the darkness of the world? Indeed, once the crop is ripe where is the need of rain-bearing clouds?

Stotra 20:
O Lord! No other deity has your pure, incessant and complete knowledge. Indeed, glass pieces glittering in a beam of light cannot match the luster and brilliance of priceless gems.

Stotra 21:
O Supreme Lord! I have seen other mundane deities before discovering you; my discontent with them has been removed by the glimpse of your detached and serene

visage. Having witnessed the Ultimate I cannot be satisfied with anything less in this or later lives.

Stotra 22:
O Unique One! There are myriad stars and planets in all directions but the sun rises only in the East. Similarly myriad women bear sons, but only one woman bore an illustrious son such as you; you are unique.

Stotra 23:
O sage of sages! All savants believe you to be Supreme, beyond the darkness of ignorance, brilliant as the sun, free of the malignance of attachment and aversion. Perceiving, understanding, and following the path of purity you have shown, leads one to immortality. There is no other path to salvation.

Stotra 24:
Lord! Seeing your different aspects, the sages address you as Amaranthine, All-Pervading, Unfathomable, Infinite, Progenitor, Perpetually Blissful, Majestic, Eternal, Serene, Lord of Ascetics, Preceptor of Yoga, Multidimensional, Unique, Omniscient and Pure.

Stotra 25:
O Jina! The wise have highly praised you as all-knowing, so you are Buddha. You are the highest patron of all beings in the cosmos, so you are Shankara. You are prime mover of the canons of Right Faith, Right Knowledge and Right Conduct, leading to Moksha, so you are Brahma. You dwell

in the thoughts of devotees in all the splendor of the Ultimate, so you are Vishnu. Hence you are Supreme.

Stotra 26:
O Deliverer from all the miseries of the Three Realms! I bow to you. O Virtuous Adored One of this World! I bow to you. O Lord Paramount of the Three Realms! I bow to you. O Terminator of the endless cycles of rebirth! I bow to you.

Stotra 27:
O Virtuous One! It is no wonder that all virtues combine and concentrate in you, leaving no room for vices. The vices have crept into myriad other beings. Inflated with false pride, they drift from the righteous path and cannot approach you even in their dreams.

Stotra 28:
O Tirthankara! Seated under the Ashoka tree, radiating your aura, you look as divinely splendid as the sun's orb amid dense clouds, piercing the darkness with its rays.

Stotra 29:
O Tirthkanra! Seated on a throne bathed in the hues of myriad gems, your lustrous golden body glows like the rising sun on the peak of the eastern mountain, emitting golden rays beneath the deep blue canopy above.

Stotra 30:
O Tirthankara! The snow-white whisks of loose fibers swinging on both sides of your golden body appear like

streams of water, pure and glittering as the rising moon, flowing down the slopes of the golden Mount Sumeru.

Stotra 31:
O Tithankara! The three-tiered canopy over your head has the soft glow of the moon. Adorned with pearl frills, it screens the sun's scorching rays. Indeed this canopy symbolizes your supremacy over the Three Realms.

Stotra 32:
Deep, resonant drum beats fill all space to hail your serene presence, to call upon all beings of Three Realms to follow the pious path you have shown. The universe resounds with this edict of the vitory of the true religion.

Stotra 33:
O Tirthankara! The divine spray of perfume and shower of fragrant flowers such as Mandara, Sunder, Nameru and Parijata waft toward you with the gentle breeze, as if your pious words have become flowers and are showered on earthlings.

Stotra 34:
O Tirthankara! Your splendorous halo is more luminous than any bright object in the universe. It dispels the darkness of night and dazzles more than many suns put together, yet it cools and soothes like the bright full moon.

Stotra 35:
O Tirthankara! Your divine voice has the power to reveal the path of liberation to all beings. Its clarity unravels the

mystery of matter and its transformation. Profound yet lucid, it flows forth in language understood by every being.

Stotra 36:
O Jina! Your feet glow like fresh golden lotuses, with their comely, sparkling nails. Wherever you step on the gods create divine golden lotuses.

Stotra 37:
O Lord of Ascetics! The height of eloquence, lucidity and eruditeness evident in your discourse is not seen anywhere else. Indeed, the darkness dissipating dazzle of the sun can never be seen in the twinkling stars and planets.

Stotra 38:
O Jina! The devotees who have submitted to you are fearless of standing face to face with an angry Elephant as large as Airavat, enraged by the buzzing of bees. The power of their deep meditation pacifies the most oppressive of the beings.

Stotra 39:
O Jina! Even an ferocious Lion Which has ripped open and shattered the forehead of an elephant, Scattering bright pearls of bone Dripping with blood to the ground, does not attack the one who has sought to shelter of your feet.

Stotra: 40:
O Jina! The world-ending Fire which scatters burning embers into the skies and threatens to engulf the whole world is extinguished in an instant by the recital of your name.

Stotra 41:
O Benevolent! A devotee who has absorbed the anti-toxin of your pious name is fearless of an approaching Snake, its eyes like red jewels, its body pitch black, its hood raised in rage.

Stotra 42:
O Conqueror of Vices! Just as darkness recedes with the rising of the sun, Armies of brave and chivalrous kings with horses and trumpeting elephants, retreat when your pious name is chanted.

Stotra 43:
O Vanquisher of Passions! In a fierce Battle where brave warriors are eager to plod over the streams of blood gushing out of the bodies of wounded elephants, the devotee who has taken shelter at your lotus feet remains invincible and embraces victory ultimately.

Stotra 44:
O Equanimous! Those who remember your name aboard a ship that is caught on the crests of giant Waves in an ocean infested with aggressive crocodiles, sharks and giant oceanic creatures dispels anxiety and delivers one to safety

Stotra 45:
O Omniscient! An extremely Sick Person, suffering from incurable diseases and having lost all hopes of recovery and survival, are cured and become as beautiful as Adonis, when they anoint the nectar-like dust taken from your lotus feet to their bodies.

Stotra 46:

O Liberated Soul! One who is in Prison, shackled form head to toe with heavy chains, whose thighs have been bruised by the rough edges of the chain links, is unshackled and freed from this bondage simply by chanting your holy name.

Stotra 47:

O Jina! The wise who recites this Hymn with devotion to your divine name will always be free from the fears of mad elephants, ferocious lions, forest fire, poisonous snakes, tempestuous oceans, fatal diseases and bondage. In fact, fear itself is afraid of him.

Stotra 48:

O Jina! With devotion I have made up this garland of your virtues. I have decorated it like a beautiful garland of color-ful flowers. Whoever recites these verses full of your virtues, with true devotion, gets the glory of the heavens and lib-eration. O Salutary God! This garland of your fine attributes has been composed by Manatunga. One who remembers this Stotra will attract the goddess Lakshmi.

Appendix C
Teachings of the Gita

The *Gita*, through the ages, has been the greatest single source of spiritual knowledge of the Indians. Although presented by scholar Vyasa as a part of the *Mahabharata*, an Indian epic, it is spoken by Lord Krishna and is looked upon as a complete work of scripture.

For many it has been a support in moments of distress, and for many it has been the light or guide for attaining a higher consciousness. Like another dispensing of food to children according to their capacity to absorb, the *Gita* has revealed the Truth to the seekers according to the maturity of their understanding: It has failed none.

It might appear surprising that a spiritual message of such untold importance should be delivered in the battlefield on the eve of a terrible war, just when two camps were ready to pounce on each other. Could not Providence have chosen a more suitable situation for the dialogue between Lord Krishna and Arjuna, who was forced to fight his cousins?

Spiritual Revelation

But in this situation itself is hidden a clue to the far-reaching significance of the *Gita*: There is no situation, no moment, which cannot turn into an opportunity for a momentous spiritual revelation. Nothing in life is outside the scope of the transforming power of the Divine.

The next question that might arise in the mind of one who has yet to study the *Gita* is: How is it that Lord

Krishna, the incarnation of God, is urging Arjuna to fight when the latter is reluctant to do so? Is peace not preferable to war? Is nonviolence not preferable to violence? If Arjuna is ready to go without such gains of war as power and wealth, should he not be encouraged in this attitude?

The *Gita* contains the answers to these questions, but in order to appreciate the answers, one has to be aware of the complex nature of human life.

Contradictory Pulls

Man is not a single entity. He is a composition of several elements such as his body, life, mind, and soul. Often a battle goes on within him when two emotions or two attractions pull him in opposite directions or when the body desires to have something while the mind refuses to support it, or when one sense of duty conflicts with another. Also there is a battle going on within a conscious man between the elements of greed, ignorant attachment, lust, etc. on the one hand, and the elements that uplift him— his aspiration to lead a pure and truthful life.

The battle that goes on outside one's self is obvious— the battle between the forces of falsehood and those of truth. In the collective life, it often expresses itself through a physical strife between two camps. This does not mean that the camp that champions the cause of truth is made up solely of pure individuals and the camp representing the falsehood is made up of those who are entirely evil. However, if love and regard for a higher ideal dominate a camp, that camp receives the support of the divine, while those dominated in their blind passion by falsehood receive the support of the darker forces. This is a universal law. The mythology describes this conflict as the battle between the *Devas* and the *Asuras*, that is, good and bad people.

The Mahabharata War, the backdrop of the *Gita*, also represents this conflict. Lord Krishna supports the Pandavas, who champion the ideas of the *Dharma* (righteousness) against the Kauravas who have become the channels for the hostile Asuric powers craving to possess the world.

To establish the order of Dharma for all humanity is Lord Krishna's mission, but that is not the sole purpose of his incarnation. To enlighten individuals who are ready within with divine secrets, is the other purpose. Arjuna is fit enough to receive the secret.

For thousands of years, those souls who are developed enough have also been initiated to the secrets through the message that was delivered to Arjuna.

What is the essence of that message?

Ulimate Purpose

Life is not meant to be spent as a plaything of *prakriti* (nature), to be tossed about like a tiny ball on the violent waves of passions, hopes, and frustrations; birth, procreation, and death. Life's ultimate purpose is to realize God.

As long as one does not know this, one lives a life by superficial standards, guided by values that are unreal. It is through numerous shocks of disillusionment that awakening comes to him. His inner being begins to guide him along the path of the true values leading to the true goal of life.

Ordinarily, one identifies oneself with one's body, mind, or life, or with a clumsy assortment of these three, but not with the soul, whereas one's true self is one's soul. It is this false identification, resulting in what is termed the ego, that works as the agent of ignorance. One feels proud, angry, offended, revengeful—all with a false self as the center. The process of the discovery of the true self continues along with the seeker's efforts to combat his ego.

This is not an easy combat. Nature, *prakriti,* through its different modes, can prove infinitely crafty and tricky. In a thousand ways, it can cloud the consciousness, make the seeker forget whatever light he has seen, and lure him back to old grooves he thought he had left behind. It is only a determined self-giving to the Divine, a continuous offering of all one does, all one thinks, and all one is to the Divine, that can ensure the seeker's continuation on the right track.

This continuous offering—the *yajna* or sacrifice, is of supreme importance. When one is no longer a slave of his ego, one is liberated from the influence of nature, he goes beyond even the *sattava,* the highest mode of nature, which inspires one to be ethical and moral. No ideal made by mind, however great and lofty, can bind him any longer. His only ideal is the Supreme Lord. The seeker lives for Him, works for Him, gathers knowledge for Him. Work, knowledge, devotion, love—the seeker cultivates all only for His Sake. To the Lord he dedicates all. His entire life becomes the *yoga*—the process of union with Him.

Determined Self-giving

Needless to say, a seeker living and working in this spirit expects no fruit from his action, as an ordinary man does. Not only the fruits of his work belong to the Divine, but also he is above the consciousness that he is the worker. He is only an instrument of the Divine—a detached worker at most.

A question arises: Can one continue with one's work when one is devoid of all desires? Accustomed as we are in our egoistic way of life to expect results from our actions—a desired result making us unhappy—the doubt becomes formidable.

But the *Gita* assures us that egoless action is always possible. Work in a spirit of equanimity, bliss, and with full surrender to the Divine can always be resorted to. As Shri Aurobindo, a noted Indian philosopher, puts the message of Lord Krishna, "I demand of you not a passive consent to a mechanical movement of Nature from which in yourself you are wholly separated, indifferent, and aloof, but action complete and Divine, done for God in you and others and for the good of the world…Action is part of the integral knowledge of God and of his greater mysterious truth and of an entire living in the Divine; action can and should be continued even after perfection and freedom are won."

Inner Renunciation

It is true that the world is full of obscurity and falsehood. It is not unusual for the seekers of truth, out of their disgust for the world, to take *sanyas*—to embrace asceticism. But according to the *Gita* the world is as much, if not more, a fit place for non-ascetics as well. What really matters is *tyaga*, the inner renunciation, not *sannyas,* an outer asceticism.

Once the seeker has got rid of his ego-self and has discovered his soul, he will know what is required of him, the path he should take, and the work he should accomplish. In other words, he will know what his *swadharma* (religious self-pursuit) is. No other moral, social, ethical, or religious duty can then be greater to him than the need to follow his *swadharma*. This is one of the cardinal doctrines of the *Gita*. For there are duties and duties. To be devoted to one's family is a duty. To sacrifice the needs of the family for the sake of the community or the country is also a duty. To be faithful to a friend is a duty; to be faithful to an ideology which the friend opposed could be yet another duty. To state the facts is an obligation; to suppress the facts and thereby save some worthy lives could be yet another obligation.

The mind does not know what is true according to the highest—the Divine—design of things. Hence it is not by a mental decision, but by the dictate of the inner voice—the voice of *swadharma*—that the seeker must dare choose his course of action.

For a while Arjuna's consciousness has been clouded by his egoistic promptings which appear moral and ideal—that he is willing to forego the promised trophies of victory for the sake of peace. But that is not the voice of his *swahdarma*. To fight is not his duty simply because he is a *Kshatriya*, the fighting class, dedicated to the right cause, but because his soul has chosen the Divine or has been chosen by the Divine to act in a certain role. He is blessed that the Divine Guide is available to him. All his mental doubts about the prevailing systems, about the concept of duty, questions about fate and freewill, are answered. Over and above that his true self is discovered to him.

By and by the Divine Guide leads Arjuna to the Supreme Secret:

Abondon all dharmas (duties) and take refuge in me alone. I will deliver thee from all sin and evil, do not grieve.

This is advice that could not have been imparted to a lesser man. A social or religious or moral code of conduct is necessary for an average man so that he does not run amok with his impulses. But for the seeker in whom the process of a conscious growth is in operation, level after level of codes of conduct lose their significance. He transcends them all. Ultimately, the Divine's Will helps him.

Spiritual Consciousness

So, Arjuna must fight, on one hand for the triumph of a cause that has the sanction of the Divine, and on the other hand for realizing the possibility of acting without any attachment for a certain result. It is true that war or any action that smacks of violence will be superfluous in an age when human nature would have undergone a fundamental change. But as long as the forces of violence are alive and active, to refrain from combating them at their own plane will amount to granting them a license for causing greater havoc. The *Gita* shows how even the crudest physical situations and pragmatic issues can be tackled with a spiritual consciousness.

Bibliography

Bhadrabahuvijay, M. *Guidelines of Jainism*. Mehsana: Sri Vishwa Kalyan Trust, 1986.

Bhargava, D. *Jaina Ethics*. Delhi: Motilal Banarsidass, 1968.

Bhattacharya, H. *Jain Moral Doctrine*. Bombay: Jain Sahitya Vikasa Mandala, 1976.

Bhattacharya, H. *Jaina Philosophy, Historical Outline*. New Delhi: Munshiram Manoharlal, 1976.

Brahmachariji, S. (translator). *Atmasiddhi-Shastra by Shrimad Raychandbhai*, 1952.

Bruhn, K. *The Jina-Images of Deogarh*. Leiden, The Netherlands: E. J. Brill, 1979.

Caillat, C., A.N. Upadhye and B.Patil, *Jainism*. Delhi: MacMillan Company of India, 1974.

Carrithers, M. and C. Humphrey (eds.). *The Assembly of Listeners: Jains in Society*. New Delhi: Cambridge University Press, 1991.

Chakraborti, H. *Asceticism in Ancient India*. Calcutta: Punthi Pustak, 1973.

Choprha, C. *A Short History of the Terapanthi Sect of The Swetamber Jains and Its Tenets*.

Calcutta: Sri Jain Swetamber Terapanthi Mahasabha, 1949.

Choprha, C. *Comparative Study of Jainism and Buddhism*. New Delhi: Sri Satguru Publications, 1982.

Dixit, K.K. *Early Jainism*. Ahmedabad: L. D. Institute of Ideology, 1978.

Dixit, K.K. (translator). *Tattvartha Sutra by Acharya Umasvati*. Ahmedabad: L. D. Institute of Ideology, 1985.

Doshi, M. *Essence of Jainism*. Chicago: India Memorial Trust, 1994.

Doshi, S. (ed.). *Homage to Shravana Belgola*. Bombay: Marg Publication, 1981.

Doshi, S. *Masterpieces of Jain Painting*. Bombay: Marg Publication, 1985.

———. *The Iconic and the Narrative in Jain Painting*. Bombay: MARG, 1972.

Dundas, P. *The Jains*. New York: Routledge, 1992.

Fischer, E. and J. Jain, *Art and Rituals: 2500 Years of Jainism*. New Delhi: Sterling Publishers, 1977.

Folkert, K.W. *Jainism: A New Handbook of Living Religions*, 2nd rev. ed. Oxford: Blackwell, 1996.

Gandhi, V.R. *Religion and Philosophy of the Jainas*. Ahmedabad: Lalit Shah Jain International Trust, 1993.

Gasenapp, H.V. *Jainism: An Indian Religion of Salvation*. Delhi: Motilal Banarsidass, 1998.

Ghosh, A. (ed.). *Tirthankara Mahavira*. New Delhi: Bharatiya Jnanpith Publications, 1975.

Gopalan, S. *Outlines of Jainism*. New Delhi: Wiley Eastern, 1973.

Green, P. *Alexander of Macedon, 356–323 B.C.: A Historical Biography*. Berkeley, CA: University of California Press, 1992.

Jacobi, H. *Jaina Sutras: Sacred Books of the East*, volumes 22 and 45. New Delhi: Oxford University Press, 1884, 1895.

Jain, C.R. *Fundamentals of Jainism*. Meerut: Veer Nirvan Bharati, 1974.

Jain, J. *Religion and Culture of the Jains*. New Delhi: Bharatiya Jnanpith Publications, 1975.

Jain, J.P. *Religion and Culture of the Jains*. New Delhi: Bharatiya Jnanapith Publications, 1988.

———. *Religion and Culture of the Jains*. New Delhi: Bharatiya Jnanpith Publications, 1983.

Jain, K.C. *Jainism in Rajasthan*. Sholapur: Gulabchand Hirachand Doshi, Jaina Samskrti Samrakshaka Sangha, 1963.

———. *Lord Mahavira and His Times*. Delhi: Motilal Banarsidass, 1974.

Jain, P.S. and V.P. Bhatt. *Bhagwan Mahavir and His Relevance in Modern Times.* Bikaner: Akhil Bharatavarshiya Sadhumargi Jain Sangha, 1976.

Jain, S.K. (ed.). *Glimpses of Jainism*. Delhi: Motilal Banarsidass, 1997.

Jaini, J.L. *Outlines of Jainism*. New Delhi: Cambridge University Press, 1916.

Jaini, P.S. *The Jaina Path of Purification*. Berkeley: University of California Press, 1979.

Johnson, W.J. *Harmless Souls-Karmic Bondage and Religious Change in Early Jainism with Special Reference to Umasvati and Kundakunda*. Delhi: Motilal Banarsidass, 1995.

Kumar, A.S. *Song of the Soul: An Introduction to the Namokar Mantra and the Science of Sound*. Blairstown, NJ: Siddhachalam Publishers, 1987.

Lanoy, R.. *The Speaking Tree: A Study of Indian Culture and Society*. London: Oxford University Press, 1974.

Lawani, K.C. *Kalpa Sutra of Bhadrabahueiden Swami*. Delhi: Motilal Banarsiddas, 1979.

———. *Uttaradhyayana: The Last Testament of Bhagavan Mahavira*. Calcutta: Prajnanam, 1977.

Marett, P. *Jainism Explained*. London: Jain Samaj Europe Publications, 1985.

Matilal, B.K. *The Central Philosophy of Jainims (Anekanta-Vada)*. Ahmedebad: L. D. Institute of Ideology, 1981.

Mehta, M.L. *Jaina Culture.* Varanasi: P. V. Research Institute, Jainashram, Hindu University, 1969.

———. *Jaina Psychology.* Armritsar: Sohanlal Jaindharma Pracharak Samiti, 1955.

Mehta, T.V. *The Path of Arhat: A Religious Democracy.* Sodhapitha: Pujya Sohanalal Smaraka Parshvanath, 1972.

Montague, A. (ed.). *Learning Non-aggression.* New York: Oxford University Press, 1978.

Mookerji, S. *The Jaina Philosophy of Non-Absolutism,* 2nd ed. Delhi: Motilal Banarsidass, 1978.

Muni Shastri, D.M. *Source-Book in Jaina Philosophy.* Udaipur: Sri Tarak Guru Jain Granthalaya, 1983.

Padmarajiah, Y.J. *Jaina Theories of Reality and Knowledge.* Bombay: Jaina Sahitya Vikas Mandala, 1963.

Pande, G.C. *Jain Thought and Culture.* Jaipur: University of Rajasthan, 1979.

Parmaj, D.S. *Light of Jain Teaching,* 2nd ed. Bahubali (Kolhapur): Sanmati Prakashan Publishers, 1981.

Prabhupada, B.S. *Higher Taste: A Guide to Gourmet Vegetarian Cooking and a Karma-Free Diet.* Los Angeles, CA: The Bhaktivedanta Book Trust, 1991.

Rampuria, C. *The Cult of Ahimsa (A Jain View-point).* Calcultta: Sri Jain Swetamber Terapanthi Mahasabha, 1947.

Ramappa, K. (translator). *Ganadhar-vad by Acharya Shri Bhuvan-bhanuji Surishvarji.* Mehsana, India: Shri Bishva Kalyan Prakashan Trust, 1987.

Ramappa, K. (translator). *A Handbook of Jainology by Acharya Shri Bhuvan-Bhanuji.* Mehsana, India: Shri Bishva Kalyan Prakshan Trust, 1987.

Sancheti, A.L. *First Steps To Jainism.* Jodhpur: M. Sujan Mal Ugam Kanwar Sancheti Trust, 1975.

Sangave, V.A. *Aspects of Jaina Religion*. New Delhi: Bhartiya Jnanpith Publications, 1990.

———. *Jaina Community: A Social Survey*, 2nd rev. ed. Bombay: Popular Prakashan, 1980.

———. *The Jaina Path of Ahisma*. Sholapur: Padmashri Sumatibai Vidyapith Trust, 1991.

Schubring, W. *The Doctrine of the Jainas*. (Translation from the rev. German ed. by Wolfgang Beurlen). Delhi: Motilal Banarsidass, 1962.

Sen, A. *The Argumentative Indian*. New York: Farrar, Straus & Giroux, 2005.

Shah, H. (editor). *Primary Principles of Jainism*. San Francisco: Jain Society of San Francisco, 1998.

Shah, H. *Jain Theism*. Ahmedabad: Academy of Philosophy, 1997.

Shah, N. (translator). *Jain Darshan (Jain Philosophy and Religion) by Muni Shri Nyayavijayaji*. New Delhi: Motilal Banarasidas, 1997.

Shanta, N. *The Unknown Pilgrims: History, Spirituality, Life of the Jaina Women Ascetics*. New Delhi: Shri Staguru Publications, 1997.

Singh, J.P. *Aspects of Early Jainism*. Banaras: Banaras Hindu University, 1972.

Singhvi, L.M. "The Jain Declaration on Nature," a paper presented to His Royal Highness Prince Philip, on October 23, 1990 at Buckingham Palace.

Sogani, K.C. *Ethical Doctrines in Jainism*. Sholapur: Lalchand Hirachand Doshi Jaina Samskrti Samrakshaka Sangha, 1967.

Stevenson, S. *The Heart of Jainism*. New Delhi: Munshiram Manoharlal, 1970.

Talib, G.S. (ed.). *Jainism*. Patiala: Punjabi University, 1975.

Tatia, N. *Studies in Jaina Philosophy*. Banaras: P. V. Research Institute, 1951.

Tobias, M. and H. Drasdo (eds.). *The Mountain Spirit*. New York: Overlook Press/Viking/

Penguin, 1979.

Todarmal, P. *Moksha Marg Prakashak*. Songadh: Swadhyay Mandir Trust, 1961.

Tobias, M. *Life Force: The World of Jainism*. San Francisco: Asian Humanities Press, 1991.

Tukol, T.K. *Compendium of Jainism*. Dharwad: Karnatak University, 1980.

———. *Yoga, Meditation & Mysticism in Jainism*. New Delhi: Raj Krishen Jain Trust, 1978.

Tulsi, A. *Illuminator Of Jaina Tenets: Jaina-Siddhanta-Dipika*. Ladnun: Jain Vishva Bharati, 1985.

———. *On Contemporary Problems*. Ladnun: Jain Vishva Bharati, 1993.

Williams, R. *Jaina Yoga*. Delhi: Motilal Banarsidass, 1983.

Made in the USA
Lexington, KY
06 August 2015